SELECTED NOBEL LAUREATES' PRIZE ACCEPTANCE SPEECHES

WITH BIOGRAPHICAL SKETCH

PEACE

ECONOMICS

LITERATURE

Dr. Gagan Jain, D.Litt.

MG BOOKS

NEW DELHI (INDIA)

SELECTED
NOBEL LAUREATES' PRIZE ACCEPTANCE SPEECHES

WITH BIOGRAPHICAL SKETCH

Published by

MG BOOKS

An Imprint of

MAANU GRAPHICS

MAANU GRAPHICS
(PUBLISHERS OF GENERAL BOOKS)
5FF, Ganpati Bhawan, 21 Ansari Road,
Darya Ganj, New Delhi-110002
Ph: 65285220, 64138266
E-mail : maanugraphics@yahoo.com
mgbooks.maanu@yahoo.com

Printed at
Satyam Enterprises, Delhi

CONTENTS

PEACE

ECONOMICS

LITERATURE

PEACE

THEODORE ROOSEVELT
1906

INTRODUCTION

Theodore Roosevelt (October 27, 1858–January 6, 1919) was born in New York. At eighteen he entered Harvard College and spent four years there, dividing his time between books and sport and excelling at both. After leaving Harvard he studied in Germany for almost a year and then immediately entered politics. He was elected to the Assembly of New York State, holding office for three years and distinguishing himself as an ardent reformer.

In 1884, because of ill health and the death of his wife, Roosevelt abandoned his political work for some time. In 1886 Roosevelt returned to New York, married again, and once more plunged into politics. In 1897 he joined President McKinley's administration as assistant secretary of the Navy. He won great fame as leader of these «Rough-Riders», whose story he told in one of his most popular books.

Elected governor of the state of New York in 1898, he invested his two-year administration with the vigorous and businesslike characteristics which were his hallmark. He would have sought reelection in 1900, since much of his work was only half done, had the Republicans not chosen him as their candidate for the second office of the Union. He held the vice-presidency for less than a year, succeeding to the presidency after the assassination of President McKinley on September 14, 1901. In 1904 Roosevelt was elected to a full term as president.

In June, 1905, President Roosevelt offered his good offices as mediator between Russia and Japan, asking the belligerents to nominate plenipotentiaries to negotiate on the conditions of peace. In August they met at Portsmouth, New Hamsphire, and after some weeks of difficult negotiations concluded a peace treaty in September, 1905. Roosevelt's candidate for president, William Howard Taft, took office in 1909. Dissatisfied with Taft's performance, Roosevelt bolted the regular Republican Party in 1912 and accepted the presidential nomination by the Progressive Party. He outpolled Taft, but Woodrow Wilson outpolled each of them. In 1917 Wilson refused his offer to raise and command a division to fight in World War I.

Roosevelt was an historian, a biographer, a statesman, a hunter, a naturalist, an orator. His prodigious literary output includes twenty-six books, over a thousand magazine articles, thousands of speeches and letters. In 1919, at the age of sixty, he died in his sleep.

PRIZE ACCEPTANCE SPEECH

Acceptance by Herbert H.D. Peirce, American Envoy.

Since President Roosevelt was not present at the award ceremony on December 10, 1906, Mr. Herbert H.D. Peirce, American envoy extraordinary and minister plenipotentiary to Norway, accepted the prize on his behalf. Mr. Peirce's speech, which included the reading of a telegram from the President, follows:

I deeply regret that my residence in your capital has been as yet too brief to enable me to address you in your own vigorous language. But "had I a thousand several tongues", they would be inadequate to express to you the deep emotion with which I appear before you to receive, on behalf of the President of the United States, this distinguished testimonial of your recognition of those acts which stamp him as preeminent in devotion to the cause of peace and goodwill on earth.

I will not vainly attempt, by any words of mine, to add to the lustre of the name of Theodore Roosevelt. His acts proclaim him, and you, Gentlemen of the Norwegian Storting, by this award of the Nobel Peace Prize, a foundation conceived in God-like love of mankind, have blazoned to the world your recognition of his wise use of his great office in the best interests of humanity.

I quote President Roosevelt's words in a telegram from him, recently received by me, when I say that he regards the award of this prize as one of the greatest honors which any man, in any position, throughout the world, can receive.

Speaking for my countrymen, I may say that this award will deeply appeal to the hearts of our people and knit closer those bonds of sympathy which unite us in the brotherhood of nations.

To me, who have enjoyed the inestimable privilege of witnessing in the course of current affairs the earnest desire with which the chief magistrate of my country is imbued to promote the cause of peace, in the interest of all mankind, when peace comports with that honorable self-respect which nations as well as individuals owe to themselves, this award seems most markedly felicitous, and I rejoice greatly in the good fortune which permits me to be the medium of transmission of this token of your appreciation of the profound love for, and lofty sense of duty to his fellowmen which is the guiding principle of his official life.

The President has directed me to read to you, Mr. President, the following message which he has telegraphed to me for that purpose:

"I am profoundly moved and touched by the signal honor shown me through your body in conferring upon me the Nobel Peace Prize. There is no gift I could appreciate more and I wish it were in my power fully to express my gratitude. I thank you for it, and I thank you on behalf of the United States; for what I did, I was able to accomplish only as the representative of the nation of which, for the time being, I am president.

After much thought, I have concluded that the best and most fitting way to apply the amount of the prize is by using it as a foundation to establish at Washington a permanent industrial peace committee. The object will be to strive for better and more equitable relations among my countrymen who are engaged, whether as capitalists or as wage workers, in industrial and agricultural pursuits. This will carry out the purpose of the founder of the prize, for in modern life it is as important to work for the cause of just and righteous peace in the industrial world as in the world of nations.

I again express to you the assurance of my deep and lasting gratitude and appreciation.

Theodore Roosevelt"

Mr. Knudsen then read the telegram in Norwegian, adding the following concluding remarks : "I am convinced, Gentlemen, that the words expressed here by the President of the United States and the aim for which he proposes to work, with the aid of the Peace Prize just awarded him, will gain worldwide approbation. It is incontrovertible, as President Roosevelt says, that peace in all its aspects, peace among mankind, peace between nations, peace between social classes, peace between individuals - all are equally important. The one cannot, so to speak, be divorced from the other. If we are to promote civilization and the well-being of mankind as a whole, we can do it most effectively by securing world peace, for the entire history of the world teaches us that war and devastation are inseparable. The ravages of war arrest the progress of nations culturally, materially, socially, and politically, perhaps for generations. This is why Alfred Nobel has by his testament erected a memorial that will live forever in the minds of men and that establishes him as one of the greatest benefactors of mankind."

SIR AUSTEN CHAMBERLAIN
1925

INTRODUCTION

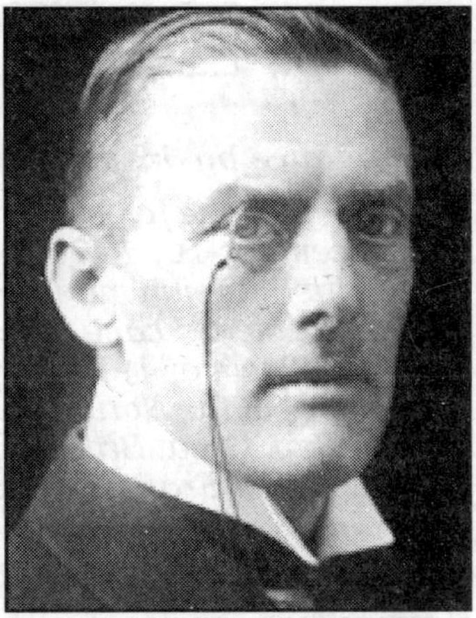

Sir Joseph Austen Chamberlain (October 16, 1863-March 17, 1937) was the eldest son of Joseph Chamberlain, the great British statesman known as the «Empire-builder» he was a half-brother of Neville Chamberlain, prime minister from 1937 to 1940. Like William Pitt the Younger, son of a famous father a hundred years earlier, he was trained for statesmanship. Upon his father's death in 1914, Austen became the member for West Birmingham, holding this seat until his own death in 1937.

Austen Chamberlain's forty-five year career in the House of Commons may be divided into two periods: the first from his entry into the House in 1892 to 1922 when Lloyd George resigned as prime minister; and the second from 1922 to his death in 1937.

Chamberlain made his mark quickly. His maiden speech in 1893 was praised by William Gladstone; from 1895 to 1900 he was civil lord of the Admiralty; from 1900 to 1902, financial secretary to the Treasury; for one year, 1902-1903, the postmaster general; from 1903 to 1906, he was chancellor of the Exchequer.

In the wartime coalition government formed by Herbert Asquith in 1915, Chamberlain accepted the position of secretary of state for India, resigning in 1917. When David Lloyd George formed a coalition government after the election of 1918, he made Chamberlain his chancellor of the Exchequer. Chamberlain filled this post from 1919 to 1921 with distinction, paying the enormous debts accumulated during the war, maintaining a stable currency, and strengthening the national credit.

In the Baldwin government of 1924 to 1929, Chamberlain was secretary of state for foreign affairs. Upon his return to London after the triumph at Locarno, Chamberlain was given an immense ovation, was made Knight of the Garter, and a year later, along with Stresemann and Briand, his two companions in diplomacy, was awarded the Nobel Peace Prize. On March 17, 1937, Austen Chamberlain died of apoplexy, the same affliction that had killed his father a month before World War I began.

PRIZE ACCEPTANCE SPEECH

Acceptance by Jospeh Austen Chamberlain.

The Peace Prize for 1925, reserved in that year, was awarded on December 10, 1926, half of it to Sir Austen Chamberlain, the British foreign minister, and half to Charles Gates Dawes. In Sir Austen's case, the prize recognized his work on the Locarno Pacts of 1925. Since he was not present at the award ceremony in the Norwegian Nobel Institute at Oslo, Sir Francis O. Lindley, Great Britain's minister in Oslo, accepted the prize for him. Sir Francis read the following telegram from Sir Austen:

"I should like you to express to the Chairman of the Nobel Committee my deep appreciation of the honor just done me by this award.

I had the good fortune to have, in my work, the collaboration of two statesmen both remarkable for the magnanimity of their spirit, for the independence of their judgment, and for their love of peace. Without their help I would have been able to do nothing. My feeling of gratitude for the award acknowledging my part in the common effort is heightened by the fact that the Committee has recognized in the same manner the important roles played by Mr. Briand and Mr. Stresemann. The outstanding work of the Dawes Committee, which preceded us, greatly facilitated our task, and I am proud to be associated with the distinguished American statesman whose name will always be remembered in connection with the great work of European reconstruction." Sir Austen did not deliver a Nobel lecture.

CHARLES G. DAWES
1925

INTRODUCTION

Charles Gates Dawes (August 27, 1865-April 23, 1951) pursued two careers during his lifetime, one in business and finance, the other in public service. He was at the height of his fame in both in 1926 when he was awarded the Nobel Peace Prize for 1925. He was the vice-president of the United States; he had achieved worldwide recognition for his report on German reparations in 1924; he had a secure reputation as a financier.

He received his bachelor's degree in 1884 at the age of nineteen, studied for two years in the Law School of the University of Cincinnati, and returned to Marietta to earn a master's degree.

In 1887 he moved to Lincoln, Nebraska, more to participate in the advantages of a fast-growing economy than to engage in the practice of law. In 1902, turning over to his brothers the management of the utilities, he entered the third phase of his business career, that of banking. He founded and became president of the Central Trust Company of Illinois, often referred to as the «Dawes Bank», and spent virtually full time in its management until 1917.

In 1917 Dawes received his commission as a major in the army and twenty-six months later was discharged as a brigadier general. In 1919, despite the opposition raised by his own Republican Party, he strongly urged the Congress to accept the Treaty of Versailles and the League of Nations.

In 1920, appointed to the newly inaugurated position of Director of the Budget, Dawes applied his conceptions of efficiency and unity to the reform of budgetary procedures in the United States government.

The League of Nations late in 1923 invited Dawes to chair a committee to deal with the question of German reparations. From 1924 to 1932, Dawes devoted his entire attention to public service. He was elected to the vice-presidency of the United States in 1924, serving in Office from 1925 to 1929. From June of 1929 to January of 1932, Dawes was the U.S. ambassador to Great Britain.

Dawes was a forthright man given to forthright talk. His nickname, «Hell and Maria» Dawes, came from some words uttered before a congressional committee investigating charges of waste and extravagance in the conduct of World War I. When a member of the committee asked Dawes if it was true that excessive prices were paid for mules in France, he shouted «Helen Maria, I'd have paid horse prices for sheep if the sheep could have pulled artillery to the front!»

He died of a coronary thrombosis at his Evanston home on April 23, 1951.

PRIZE ACCEPTANCE SPEECH

Acceptance by Charles Gates Dawes.

Charles Dawes, vice-president of the United States, was not present to receive the Peace Prize for 1925, which he shared with Sir Austen Chamberlain. Given in recognition of his work as chairman of the Dawes Committee handling the problem of German reparations, the award (reserved in 1925) was made on December 10, 1926, at the Nobel Institute in Oslo. The prize was accepted on his behalf by Laurits Selmer Swenson, the United States minister in Oslo, who read the following telegram from Mr. Dawes:

"This award, which is in recognition of the work of the First Committee of Experts, Reparation Commission, of which I was chairman, is gratefully acknowledged. The committee was composed of Owen D. Young, Sir Josiah C. Stamp, Sir Robert M. Kindersley, Jean Parmentier, Edgard Allix, Alberto Pirelli, Frederico Flora, Emile Francqui, Baron Maurice Houtart, and myself. It was the endeavor of the experts to found their plan upon the principles of justice, fairness, and mutual interest, relying for its acceptance thus prepared upon that common good faith which is the enduring hope for the universal safeguarding of peace. That the results achieved under it have merited in your judgment this high recognition is a tribute to the united efforts of the committee."

Mr. Dawes did not deliver a Nobel lecture.

ARISTIDE BRIAND
1926

INTRODUCTION

Aristide Briand (March 28, 1862-March 7, 1932), while at the height of his influence within the League of Nations, attended a dinner in Geneva where the guests were given menu cards on which was printed a cartoon depicting the statesmen of the world smashing a statue of Mars while Briand, alone, talked to the god of war trying to convince him to commit suicide.

Aristide Briand was born in (March 28, 1862)Brittany. His father, a prosperous innkeeper, sent him to school in Saint-Nazaire and then to the Nantes Lycée.

Although Briand studied law and established a practice, he preferred the profession of journalism to that of law. He wrote for *Le Peuple, La Lanterne, La Petite République*, and collaborated with Jean Jaurès in founding *L'Humanité*, a socialist paper.

He guided the legislation through the Chamber and in 1906 was appointed to administer the law itself as minister of public instruction and worship in Sarrien's cabinet. He was retained in this post when Clemenceau formed a government later in that year, was given the justice portfolio in Clemenceau's next government, and in 1909 became premier for the first time.

Briand tended to be a political loner. In 1906 when he joined Sarrien's government, he was expelled from the Socialist Party. Briand, the enemy of war, was forced by the irony of events to lead his nation during World War I for eighteen critical months from October, 1915, to March, 1917.

Briand was not a member of the Clemenceau government

which conducted the negotiations for France at Versailles after the war. When he resumed as premier in January of 1921, retaining for himself the portfolio for foreign affairs, he tried to obtain a settlement of the reparations issue; represented France at the Washington Arms Conference; and negotiated a security pact with Lloyd George at Cannes in 1922, resigning when he failed to obtain its ratification.

Recalled to the foreign ministry by Painlevé in 1925, Briand now entered upon five and a half years of highly successful diplomacy. The last major proposal Briand offered to the world was his sweeping concept of a European Union outlined in a memorandum to twenty-six nations in May, 1930. In September the proposal was presented to the League of Nations, but when Briand was not reappointed to the foreign ministry after Premier Laval's resignation in January, 1932, the proposal languished.

Briand died quite unexpectedly on March 7, 1932; he was buried at Cocherel, his country retreat.

PRIZE ACCEPTANCE SPEECH

Acceptance by Aristide Briand.

Mr. Briand, the French foreign minister, who shared with Gustav Stresemann the Peace Prize for 1926 - awarded because of their contributions to the Locarno Pacts the year before - was not present at the presentation ceremony in Oslo on December 10, 1926. The French chargé d'affaires, J. Billebault du Chaffault, accepted the prize in his behalf and read the following telegram from Mr. Briand:

"The Norwegian Government kindly informed me through its distinguished representative in Paris that the eminent body responsible for awarding the Nobel Peace Prize had conferred it on General Dawes, Sir Austen Chamberlain, Mr. Stresemann, and on me. I am anxious to express to it my profound gratitude for the great honor done me. No recognition could be more precious to me than this which now crowns the most important effort of my public life, one I have dedicated in every way within my power to the realization of your ideal of peace."

Mr. Briand did not deliver a Nobel lecture.

ARTHUR HENDERSON
1934

INTRODUCTION

Arthur Henderson (September 13, 1863-October 20, 1935) was born in Glasgow, the son of David Henderson, a manual worker. When his father died in 1872, leaving the family in poverty, Arthur left school to work in a photographer's shop.

In the course of his work in the Methodist church, which he had joined as a young man, Henderson met Eleanor Watson and married her in 1888. In 1896 he moved his family to Darlington; there, he was elected to the Durham County Council and in 1903 became the first Labor mayor of Darlington.

In 1917 he went to Russia as an official observer for the British government; in 1918 he broke with Lloyd George over his refusal to send delegates to a proposed international conference of socialists, a conference which, as it turned out, was never convened. In 1924 he was home secretary in MacDonald's cabinet, but spent most of his energy on two international problems: the implementation of the Dawes Plan for German reparations and the drafting of the Geneva Protocol on the ultimate settlement of international disputes by arbitration.

In January, 1931, he prodded the Council into completing preparations for the calling of a Disarmament Conference; in May of that year, he was unanimously approved as president of the conference; on February 2, 1932, he presided over the opening session. Despite his determined and persistent work, the conference failed. The world was stricken with an economic depression; Germany, under Hitler, withdrew from the conference in October, 1933; Henderson was barely able to hold the conference together in 1934, but even as late as December of that year at the Nobel ceremonies in Oslo, he optimistically insisted that the conference was still very much alive.

Henderson was a strong man. His powerful physical presence was the outer counterpart of his inner moral integrity. He had the qualities, Clement Attlee remarked in his eulogy on Henderson in the House of Commons , needed «in a working ironworker to rise to preside over the Assembly of the nations.

PRIZE ACCEPTANCE SPEECH

Arthur Henderson's Acceptance Speech on the occasion of the award of the Nobel Peace Prize in Oslo, December 10, 1934. Your Royal Highness, Mr. Prime Minister, Mr. President, Members of the Nobel Peace Committee, and Ladies and Gentlemen:

I am deeply touched by the kind words which you, Mr. Prime Minister, have used today in introducing me to this distinguished gathering. You will, I am sure, appreciate the emotions which are evoked in me by the decision of the Trustees of the Nobel Peace Committee. I recall the names of some of the devoted servants of humanity and peace to whom this great honour has been awarded in the past - President Wilson, Dr. Nansen, Léon Bourgeois, Sir Austen Chamberlain, Dr. Stresemann, my old friends and collaborators, the late Aristide Briand and H. Branting. May I not be pardoned, therefore, if I am experiencing a deep feeling of pride that you should have thought it fit and proper to add my name to that illustrious list?

You were good enough to make special mention, Mr. Prime Minister, of the Disarmament Conference. You asked: "*Is* the Conference alive? *is* there still hope?" It would be a sad day, not only for us here but for the great masses of humble citizens in all lands, if that question had to be answered in the negative. As you have stated, Mr. Prime Minister, I have devoted nearly three years to the work of the Disarmament Conference. It has been a period of anxious and exacting labours for all - a period of difficulty and delay and disappointments - of hopes deferred. But if success has yet to be achieved, at least that decisive and heart-breaking word "failure" has not been written. And I cannot conceive that it will be allowed to be written.

I have spent a long life-time in public affairs, and I would say, without any hesitation, that there is no human issue upon which the aspirations, hopes, and yearnings of the peoples are concentrated in a greater measure than that of the achievement of a secure world peace. You, Sir, reminded us of the words of one of your distinguished compatriots, who has said that: "The thought of Peace is the greatest thought in the world". Thoughts are most fruitful in action, and I can imagine no greater or more fruitful action in the world than that which leads the peoples into the golden age of Peace and Freedom and Security. Men walk by faith and not by sight. If we have faith in humanity, in the divine spark which is in all of us, faith in the community of toil and suffering and the common struggle after a fuller and nobler life, which is mankind's heritage upon this earth, then, with courage and steadfastness of purpose, we cannot fail to achieve mankind's greatest goal - the establishment of a world brotherhood founded in Peace, Security, and Freedom.

Again I thank all concerned, and trust that with God's help I may ever prove worthy of the confidence which you have shown.

CORDELL HULL
1945

INTRODUCTION

Cordell Hull (October 2, 1871-July 23, 1955) was born in a log cabin in Pickett County, Tennessee, the third of the five sons of William and Elizabeth (Riley) Hull. He received a law degree in 1891 after completing a one-year course at Cumberland University at Lebanon, Tennessee.

From 1893 to 1897 he was a member of the Tennessee House of Representatives, abandoning politics temporarily to serve as captain of the Fourth Tennessee Regiment in the Spanish-American War. Hull returned to the practice of law, this time in Gainsboro, Tennessee, but in 1903 was appointed judge of the Fifth Judicial District. He held this position until 1907, earning the nickname «Judge», used even by his wife, Rose Frances Whitney, whom he married in 1917.

Elected to Congress from the Fourth Tennessee District in 1907, Hull served as a U.S. representative until 1931, interrupted only by two years as chairman of the Democratic National Committee.

Hull was elected U.S. senator for the 1931-1937 term but resigned upon his appointment as secretary of state by President Franklin D. Roosevelt on March 4, 1933. He was sixty-two. In 1944 when he resigned because of ill health, he had occupied this important post for almost twelve years, the longest tenure in American history.

His debut in this office was not auspicious. He headed the

American delegation to the Monetary and Economic Conference in London in July, 1933, a conference which ended in failure despite the parlous state of world prosperity. Hull was responsive, also, to the problems arising in other parts of the globe.

From 1936 on, foreseeing danger to peace in the rise of the dictators, he advocated rearmament, pled for the implementation of a system of collective security, supported aid short of war to the Western democracies, condemned Japanese encroachment into Indo-China, warned all branches of the U.S. military well in advance of the attack on Pearl Harbor to prepare to resist simultaneous, surprise attacks at various points.

Although obliged because of the precarious state of his health to resign as secretary of state in late November, 1944, Hull nonetheless served as a member of and senior adviser to the American delegation to the United Nations Conference in San Francisco in 1945.

PRIZE ACCEPTANCE SPEECH

As the Laureate was unable to be present on the occasion of the award of the Nobel Peace Prize in Oslo, December 10, 1945, the acceptance was read by Mr. Lithgow Osborne, ambassador of the United States to Norway

Your Majesty; Your Royal Highnesses; Your Excellencies, Mr. Chairman and Members of the Nobel Committee of the Storting.

I have the honor to accept, on behalf of my distinguished fellow-citizen, Mr. Cordell Hull, former Secretary of State and Father of the UNO, the Nobel Peace Prize for 1945.

I have been requested by Mr. Hull to read - on this occasion - the following message from him to the President and members of the Nobel Committee of the Storting:

As I have already informed you, the present state of my health renders impossible my presence at Oslo on this most memorable occasion. Nothing would have given me greater pleasure and satisfaction. Please let me assure you, however, that the keen disappointment and regret which I feel in this regard serve only to enhance my profound appreciation of the great honor which you have done me;

and my sincere gratitude for your generous action.

The Nobel Peace Prize has come to occupy a very special place in the thoughts - and emotions of forward-looking humanity. It has become a supreme mark of distinction in the field of effort directed toward the attainment of man's highest aspiration - the establishment of enduring peace based on justice and fair-dealing for all. I am proud to join the company of those whom you have thus far so honored.

The problem of peace is uppermost today/ in the hearts and minds of all of us, as the world emerges from the staggering ordeal of the most widespread and cruel war of all the ages. That war has brought with it a truly incredible development of means of destruction and a terrifying prospect of rapid and almost limitless development in that direction. Triumphant science and technology are only at the threshold of man's command over sources of energy so stupendous that, if used for military purposes, they can wipe out our entire civilization. Under the ominous shadow which the second World War and its attendant circumstances have cast on the world, peace has become as essential to civilized existence as the air we breathe is to life itself. There is no greater responsibility resting upon peoples and governments everywhere than to make sure that enduring peace will this time - at long last - be established *and maintained*. Fortunately, the war has brought with it not alone a stark realization of what another war would mean to the world, but as well the creation of an international agency through which the nations of the world can, if they so desire, make peace a living reality. Within a few weeks the organization for the maintenance of international peace and security, established by the San Francisco Charter, will be formally launched through the convocation of the first General Assembly of the United Nations. I fully realize that the new organization is a human rather than a perfect instrumentality for the attainment of its great objective. As time goes on it will, I am sure, be improved. The Charter is sufficiently flexible to provide for growth and development, in the light of experience and performance, but I am firmly convinced that with all its imperfections the United Nations Organization offers the peace-loving nations of the world, how, a fully workable mechanism which will give them peace, if they want peace. To be sure, no piece of social machinery, however well constructed, can be effective unless there is back of it a will and a determination to make it work. The crucial test for men and for nations today is whether or not they have suffered enough, and have learned enough, to put aside suspicion, prejudice and short-run and narrowly conceived interests and to unite in furtherance of their greatest common interest. That overwhelming and overshadowing common interest is enduring peace, within the frame-work of which man's newly found powers of science and technology can be used to raise to undreamed of heights the well-being of humanity. Alfred Nobel, were he alive today, would, I am sure, have joined with me in unshakeable faith that this crucial test will be met; that the searing lessons of this latest war and the promise of the United Nations Organization will be the cornerstones of a new edifice of enduring peace and the guideposts of a new era of human progress.

EMILY GREENE BALCH
1946

INTRODUCTION

Emily Greene Balch (January 8, 1867-January 9, 1961) was born in Boston, the daughter of Francis V. and Ellen (Noyes) Balch.

In 1896 she joined the faculty of Wellesley College, rising to the rank of professor of economics and sociology in 1913. An outstanding teacher, she impressed students by the clarity of her thought, by the breadth of her experience, by her compassion for the underprivileged, by her strong-mindedness, and by her insistence that students could formulate independent judgments only if they combined on-the-spot investigation with their research in the library.

Although Miss Balch was not a member of Henry Ford's «Peace Ship», in 1915, she was a member of his Neutral Conference for Continuous Mediation, based at Stockholm, for which she drew up a position paper called «International Colonial Administration», proposing a system of administration not unlike that of the mandate system later accepted by the League of Nations.

Returning to the United States, she campaigned actively against America's entry into the conflict. She asked for an extension of her leave of absence from the faculty of Wellesley College, but the trustees in 1918 decided instead to terminate her contract. She accepted a position on the editorial staff of the liberal weekly, the Nation; wrote Approaches to the Great Settlement, with an introduction by Norman Angell, a future

Nobel Peace Prize winner (for 1933); attended the second convention of the International Congress of Women held in Zurich in 1919 and accepted its invitation to become secretary of its operating organization WILPF, The Women's International League for Peace and Freedom, with headquarters in Geneva. This post she relinquished in 1922, but when the League was hard pressed financially in 1934, she again acted, without salary, as international secretary for a year and a half. It was to this League that Miss Balch donated her share of the Nobel Peace Prize money.

Even after receiving the Peace Prize in 1946 at the age of seventy-nine, Miss Balch continued, despite frail health, to participate in the cause to which she had given her life.

PRIZE ACCEPTANCE SPEECH

As the Laureate was unable to be present on the occasion of the award of the Nobel Peace Prize in Oslo, December 10, 1946 the acceptance was read by Gunnar Jahn, Chairman of the Nobel Committee.

I desire to express my grateful appreciation of this great honour and my pleasure in being associated in it today with Dr. John R. Mott and, earlier, with Jane Addams, with that martyr for peace and freedom, Karl von Ossietzky, and with so many others, both the publicly honored and the unknown who have served and are serving the same cause. I am happy in thinking that not I myself but the Womens' International League for Peace and Freedom, with which I am identified, is the true recipient. Hoping, as I do, that this internationally organized body of women has ahead of it a great opportunity for usefulness in educating people everywhere toward the world-mindedness on which peace must be based with other people, I am hoping that 1946 will mark a turning point in the age-old effort to rid the world of war, to national disarmament, to renunciation of power politics, and to development of international trusteeship, not only for dependent peoples, but for regions and interests which are essentially supranational in character, such as the Polar regions and the main waterways of the world, including the Mediterranean and all the great strategic canals, among them the Panama.

JOHN R. MOTT
1946

INTRODUCTION

John Raleigh Mott (May 25, 1865-January 31, 1955) was born of pioneer stock in Livingston Manor, New York, the third child and only son among four children. His parents, John and Elmira (Dodge) Mott, moved to Postville, Iowa, where his father became a lumber merchant and was elected the first mayor of the town.

In the summer of 1886, Mott represented Cornell University's Y.M.C.A. at the first international, interdenominational student Christian conference ever held. During Mott's remaining two years at Cornell, as president of the Y.M.C.A. he increased the membership threefold and raised the money for a university Y.M.C.A. building. He was graduated in 1888, a member of Phi Beta Kappa, with a bachelor's degree in philosophy and history. In September of 1888 he began a service of twenty-seven years as national secretary of the Intercollegiate Y.M.C.A. of the U.S.A. and Canada, a position requiring visits to colleges to address students concerning Christian activities.

In 1912 and 1913, he toured the Far East, holding twenty-one regional missionary conferences in India, China, Japan, and Korea.

From 1915 to 1928, Mott was general-secretary of the International Committee of the Y.M.C.A. and from 1926 to 1937 president of the Y.M.C.A.'s World Committee.

Dr. Mott married Leila Ada White of Wooster, Ohio, in 1891;

they had four children, two sons and two daughters. He died at his home in Orlando, Florida, at the age of eighty-nine.

PRIZE ACCEPTANCE SPEECH

John R. Mott's Acceptance Speech, on the occasion of the award of the Nobel Peace Prize in Oslo, December 10, 1946

Your Majesty, Your Royal Highnesses, Your Excellencies, Mr. Chairman and members of the Nobel Committee of the Storting and other friends:

I do not trust myself to voice emotions which well-nigh master me in contemplation of the signal honor conferred on me in the granting of the Nobel Peace Award, and of the gracious and generous words of the President. I appreciate deeply the high privilege of being bracketed in this presentation with Miss Emily Balch, in whose distinguished career of international helpfulness I take pride.

As the President has indicated, my life has been a life of travel - for 60 years constantly moving over the wide world on journeys which first and last have taken me to 83 countries, and, what is more significant, to most of them again and again.

In this world-wide effort I have concentrated on successive generations of youth. If I were to add a word it would be a word of abounding hope. The present new generation across the breadth of the world, and whose representatives are planning to assemble here in Norway in the coming summer to take counsel together, I can testify are responsive to the Nobel Peace ideal, and are planning, as no previous generation, for a great united advance in the furtherance of peace and good-will throughout the world.

LORD BOYD ORR
1949

INTRODUCTION

John Boyd Orr (September 23, 1880-June 25, 1971) was born in Kilmaurs, Ayrshire, Scotland. His father, R.C. Orr, was a pious and intelligent man whose sudden enthusiasms led to frequent reversals of fortune, but, although his finances were often depleted, he and his wife and their seven children enjoyed a pleasant life in their rural community. Having begun his education in the village school, John at the age of thirteen was sent to Kilmarnock Academy, twenty miles away, but he was more interested in the life of the navvies and quarrymen who worked in his father's quarry than in his education and so was returned to the village school. There he became a member of the staff as a «pupil teacher», earning £20 a year by the time he was eighteen. It was symbolic of this period of his life that he should have been informed of his Nobel Peace Prize award by his banker. The prize money, however, he donated to the National Peace Council, the World Movement for World Federal Government, and various other such organizations. John Boyd Orr, himself a scientist-adjuster of old systems, died at his home in Scotland in June, 1971, at the age of ninety.

PRIZE ACCEPTANCE SPEECH

Lord Boyd Orr's Acceptance Speech, on the occasion of the award of the Nobel Peace Prize in Oslo, December 10, 1949

Your Majesty, Mr President, Ladies and Gentlemen, no one standing in the position I am in this day, could be otherwise than embarrassed by grave doubts of being worthy to receive this Nobel Peace Prize, in my opinion, the greatest honour any man can get.

In my case the embarrassment is somewhat relieved by the thought that the award is not so much to me personally as to the movements with which I have been connected.

These are, first the one to get nations to co-operate in applying modern science to develop the vast potential resources of the earth to put an end to hunger and poverty and bring economic prosperity to the peoples of all countries. This would put an end to one of the main causes of social unrest and war, and be an important step towards international agreement and peace.

The other is the more direct though more difficult road to peace by the formation of a world government with power to replace international anarchy by international law which all countries whatever their national ideology would obey.

I hope that all those who have worked for these complementary approaches to World Unity and Peace will regard me as their representative and feel encouraged to redouble their efforts which have been sealed with the approval of the Committee making this award.

Now, may I say one word about this Nobel Peace Prize. In the past honours have been given to successful leaders in war. And, indeed, until recently, it was possible to think of glory and chivalry being associated with War. But, as Alfred Nobel foresaw the advance of science has made the former kind of war fought only by soldiers, no longer possible. There can be nothing glorious or chivalrous about a war with atomic bombs and the more terrifying biological weapons. A war with these weapons would be wholesale massacre of civilians old and young, from which few in Europe would escape, for, as has been truly said there would be "nowhere to hide".

Alfred Nobel's greatest contribution to the welfare of humanity was not high explosives which have been of great value in mining and other industries. That would have been invented soon, in any case, by some chemist. It was his prophetic foresight which enabled him to see that the advance of science would make war so disastrous that no government of sane men would consider war as a means of settling international disputes. The establishment of a prize to encourage efforts for peace was the natural outcome of this visionary of the future.

And, now, in conclusion, I wish to thank you Mr. President and the members of your Committee for the great honour you have done me in choosing me as the recipient of the Nobel Peace Prize, an honour enhanced by the presence here today of His Majesty The King and other members of The Royal Family.

RALPH BUNCHE
1950

INTRODUCTION

Ralph Johnson Bunche (August 7, 1904-1971) was born in Detroit, Michigan. His father, Fred Bunche, was a barber in a shop having a clientele of whites only; his mother, Olive (Johnson) Bunche, was an amateur musician; his grandmother, «Nana» Johnson, who lived with the family, had been born into slavery. When Bunche was ten years old, the family moved to Albuquerque, New Mexico, in the hope that the poor health of his parents would improve in the dry climate. Both, however, died two years later. His grandmother, an indomitable woman who appeared Caucasian «on the outside» but was «all black fervor inside», took Ralph and his two sisters to live in Los Angeles. Here Ralph contributed to the family's hard pressed finances by selling newspapers, serving as house boy for a movie actor, working for a carpet-laying firm, and doing what odd jobs he could find. Bunche has always been active in the civil rights movement. At Howard University he was considered by some as a young radical intellectual who criticized both America's social system and the established Negro organizations, but generally he is thought of as a moderate.

Bunche still works for the UN. From 1955 to 1967, he served as undersecretary for Special Political Affairs and since 1968 has been undersecretary-general. During these years he has taken on many special assignments. When war erupted in the Congo in 1960, Dag Hammarskjöld, then secretary-general of the UN, appointed him as his special representative to oversee the UN commitments there. He has shouldered analogous duties in Cyprus, Kashmir, and Yemen. *Ralph Bunche died on December 9, 1971.*

PRIZE ACCEPTANCE SPEECH

Ralph Bunche's Acceptance Speech, on the occasion of the award of the Nobel Peace Prize, Oslo, December 10, 1950.

Your Majesty,Your Royal Highnesses, Mr. President of the Nobel Committee, Ladies and Gentlemen,

To be honored by one's fellow men is a rich and pleasant experience. But to receive the uniquely high honor here bestowed today, because of the world view of Alfred Nobel long ago, is an overwhelming experience. To the President and members of the Nobel Committee I may say of their action, which at this hour finds its culmination, only that I am appreciative beyond the puny power of words to convey. I am inspired by your confidence.

I am not unaware, of course, of the special and broad significance of this award - far transcending its importance or significance to me as an individual - in an imperfect and restive World in which inequalities among peoples, racial and religious bigotries, prejudices and taboos are endemic and stubbornly persistent. From this northern land has come a vibrant note of hope and inspiration for vast millions of people whose bitter experience has impressed upon them that color and inequality are inexorably concomitant.

There are many who figuratively stand beside me today and who are also honored here. I am but one of many cogs in the United Nations, the greatest peace organization ever dedicated to the salvation of mankind's future on earth. It is, indeed, itself an honor to be enabled to practise the arts of peace under the aegis of the United Nations.

As I now stand before you, I cannot help but reflect on the never-failing support and encouragement afforded me, during my difficult assignment in the Near East, by Trygve Lie:, and by his Executive Assistant, Andrew Cordier. Nor can I forget any of the more than 700 valiant men and women of the United Nations Palestine Mission who loyally served with Count Bernadotte and me, who were devoted servants of the cause of peace, and without whose tireless and fearless assistance our mission must surely have failed. At this moment, too, I recall, all too vividly and sorrowfully, that ten members of that mission gave their lives in the noble cause of peace-making.

But above all, there was my treasured friend and former chief, Count Folke Bernadotte, who made the supreme sacrifice to the end that Arabs and Jews should be returned to the ways of peace. Scandinavia, and the peaceloving world at large, may long revere his memory, as I shall do, as shall all of those who participated in the Palestine peace effort under his inspiring command.

In a dark and perilous hour of human history, when the future of all mankind hangs fatefully in the balance, it is of special symbolic significance that in Norway, this traditionally peace-loving nation, and among such friendly and kindly people of great good-will, this ceremony should be held for the exclusive purpose of paying high tribute to the sacred cause of peace on earth, good-will among men. May there be freedom, equality and brotherhood among all men. May there be morality in the relations among nations. May there be, in our time, at long last, a world at peace in which we, the people, may for once begin to make full use of the great good that is in us.

LESTER BOWLES PEARSON
1957

INTRODUCTION

For four decades Lester Bowles Pearson (April 23, 1897-1972) has been noted for his diplomatic sensitivity, his political acumen, and his personal popularity. He is affectionately called «Mike», a nickname given to him by his flying instructor in World War I, who discarded «Lester» as being insufficiently bellicose.

Born in Toronto of Irish stock on both sides of his family, he received a balanced education in politics, learning the conservative position from his father, a Methodist minister, and the liberal from his mother. Pearson entered Victoria College at the University of Toronto in 1913 at the age of sixteen. Too young to enlist as a private when Canada declared war in 1914, he volunteered to serve with a hospital unit sponsored by the University. After two years in England, Egypt, and Greece, he was commissioned and transferred eventually to the Royal Flying Corps, but, sustaining some injuries from two accidents, one of them a plane crash, he was invalided home.

Pearson drafted the speech in which Prime Minister St. Laurent proposed the establishment of the North Atlantic Treaty Organization (NATO), signed the enabling treaty in 1949, headed the Canadian delegation to NATO until 1957, and functioned as chairman of the NATO Council in 1951-1952. Pearson also headed the Canadian delegation to the UN from 1946 to 1956, being elected to the presidency of the Seventh Session of the General Assembly in 1952-1953. As chairman of the General Assembly's Special Committee on Palestine, he laid the groundwork for the creation of the state of Israel in 1947.

Pearson retired from the leadership of his party in the spring of 1968 and died in 1972.

Lester Bowles Pearson died on December 27, 1972.

PRIZE ACCEPTANCE SPEECH

Lester Bowles Pearson's Acceptance Speech, on the occasion of the award of the Nobel Peace Peace Prize in Oslo, December 10, 1957

May I thank you, Mr. Chairman, for your very kind and generous words. I am sorry that I am not sufficiently educated to have understood them in Norwegian but I was able to detect two words, "Lester Pearson". They seemed to me to recur all too frequently but I suppose that in the circumstance it was hard to avoid that.

I am very conscious of the fact this morning that I have received an honour that cannot fail to arouse deep emotion in the heart of the recipient. My feeling of pride and honour is increased by the presence here today of His Majesty and Her Royal Highness and by the fact, sir, that you are presiding over the ceremonies.

I realise also that I share this honour with many friends and colleagues who have worked with me for the promotion of peace and good understanding between peoples. I am grateful for the opportunities I have been given to participate in that work as a representative of my country, Canada, whose people have, I think, shown their devotion to peace.

I am deeply aware of the fact that in receiving this honour I am entering a company of men and women who have served humanity with unselfish and constructive devotion. They include, I know, two great Norwegians, Christian Lange and Fridtjof Nansen. I feel very proud and humble at having my name now linked with such men, because of the choice that you, sir, and the members of your honourable committee have made.

I am particularly happy to be able to receive this prize in Norway, a country which has so well discharged its duty to the international community and to Peace.

Alfred Nobel, not himself a Norwegian, recognised this when he conferred on Norway through your Committee the honour and responsibility of making the Peace Award.

On this occasion I wish to pay my sincere tribute to this great Swedish man of vision and action, who worked hard, lived nobly and ensured that his influence for good would extend far beyond his own life time.

Alfred Nobel decreed that this award should be conferred on someone who, in the opinion of the Committee, should have done the most or the best work to promote fraternity between nations for the abolition and reduction of standing armies and for the holding and promotion of peace congresses.

As to the first, I do not know that I have done very much myself to promote fraternity between nations but I *do* know that there can be no more important purpose for any man's activity or interests.

So far as abolishing arms are concerned, those of Nobel's day are now out of date, but I know, as you do, that if the arms which man's genius has created today to replace them are ever used they will destroy us all. So they must be themselves destroyed.

As for the promotion of peace congresses we have had our meetings and assemblies, but the promotion through them of the determined and effective will to peace displaying itself in action and policy remains to be achieved.

Alfred Nobel - with a whimsical touch - once said:

"I would not leave anything to a man of action as he would be tempted to give up work; on the other hand, I would like to help dreamers as they find it difficult to get on in life."

Perhaps this sentiment should have a special appeal for Norwegians who, though adept in overcoming difficulties by practical action, have been described as a "people who luxuriated in the wealth of their dreams."

Of all our dreams today there is none more important - or so hard to realise - than that of peace in the world. May we never lose our faith in it or our resolve to do everything that can be done to convert it one day into reality.

The great Ibsen has one of his characters in the play "The Emperor and The Galilean" say:

"There are three Empires. First there is the Empire which was founded on the tree of knowledge. Then there is the Empire founded on the tree of the Cross. The third is still a secret Empire which will be founded on the tree of knowledge and the tree of the Cross - brought together."

The award which I have received today at this ceremony, which my wife and I will always remember with emotion, is a renewed incentive to work with all other men of good will in the world for the triumph of Ibsen's third Empire, that of the Empire of Peace.

PHILIP NOEL-BAKER
1959

INTRODUCTION

Philip John Noel-Baker (November 1, 1889-1982) is a man of strong and steadfast convictions. To a reporter who interviewed him after the Norwegian Nobel Committee announced that he had been awarded the Peace Prize, he said, «War is a damnable, filthy thing and has destroyed civilization after civilization - that is the essence of my belief.»

Noel-Baker, who formally joined his wife's surname with his own in 1943, was reared in an atmosphere of affluence, religious observance, and political activism. He was one of seven children of a Canadian-born Quaker, Joseph Allen Baker, who moved to England to establish what became a profitable machine manufacturing firm. The elder Baker was a pactfist and humanitarian who held a seat on the London County Council from 1895 to 1907 and in the House of Commons from 1905 to 1918. A stellar performer in the middle distances, he ran in the Olympic Games held in Stockholm in 1912 and captained the British track team at the 1920 Olympics in Antwerp and at the 1924 Games in Paris.

From 1914 until the present day, Noel-Baker has three times accepted academic posts but has left them to pursue a career in public service. Having completed his M.A., he accepted the post of vice-principal of Ruskin College at Oxford in 1914, but with the onset of the war, he organized and became the commandant of the Friends' Ambulance Unit attached to the fighting front in France (1914-1915) and subsequently became adjutant of the First British Ambulance Unit for Italy (1915-1918). In France he won the Mons Star (1915); in Italy, the Silver Medal for Military Valor (1917) and the Croce di Guerra (1918). In 1915 he met and married a field hospital nurse, Irene Noel, the daughter of a British landowner in Achmetaga, Greece.

Noel-Baker has continued to reside in London since the death of his wife in 1956. For about twenty years he had the pleasure of serving in the House of Commons as a colleague of his only child, Francis Noel-Baker.

Noel-Baker died in 1982.

PRIZE ACCEPTANCE SPEECH

Philip Noel-Baker's Acceptance Speech, on the occasion of the award of the Nobel Peace Peace Prize in Oslo, December 10, 1959 Your Majesty, Your Royal Highnesses, Mr. Chairman, Your Excellencies, Ladies and Gentlemen:

How can I fulfill what must always be the first duty of every man or woman who stands where I stand now?

Perhaps I can do it most simply, but most adequately, by saying that there is none in the world with whom I would exchange my place today.

There has come to me what I have always counted as the greatest of the honours which men bestow; it has come to me in the lovely capital of a beloved country, mantled now in Christmas snow; it has come by the decision of your Nobel Committee of wise and most distinguished men.

What more could any man or woman ask of Fate?

May I also express my deep gratitude for the generous hospitality with which Your Majesty, and Norway, have received me since I arrived? There is nothing in the world like a Norwegian welcome.

I am much embarrassed by the fact that after so many months as a guest in Norway over so many years, I cannot answer Mr. Gunnar Jahn in the Norwegian tongue. It is true that my friend, Toralv Öksnevad, in a dark hour of the war, not once, but twice and even thrice, made me broadcast in Norwegian to his captive compatriots at home. Desperate things are done in war-time.

But if I tried now, I should have to use the words of Sir Winston Churchill when he spoke to 100 000 Frenchmen in the streets of Paris after the City had been liberated in 1944. "Prenez garde", he said; "I am about to speak to you in French. It is a formidable undertaking, which will impose a heavy strain upon your friendship for Great Britain".

How heavy the strain could be, he once showed in an early conversation with General de Gaulle, soon after the General had raised the Free French flag in London. "Mon General", he is reported to have said, "si vous m'opposerez, je vous liquidaterai".

My excuse for speaking English now is the reason why I have never been able to learn Norwegian: I have never had the chance to try, for everyone in Norway seems to me to speak English at least as well as, and often rather better, than I do myself.

But it would be easy in any language to extol the merits of the Founder of the Nobel Prize. Alfred Nobel was, by every test, one of the great men of his own day; but the recognition of his greatness is more universal now, than when he died; we know now that he had all the passion and the vision which the world required in his time, and which it still so urgently requires today.

Nobel was a chemist; a leader in a magical new science then forging rapidly ahead; like other scientists and inventors, he discovered, without the slightest premonition on his part that it would be so, that the products of his genious could be used for war.

The General Staffs seized eagerly upon his high explosive, and used them to increase the fire-power, and the offensive power, of their armies and their fleets. Watching this rapid and competitive expansion of the military forces which the Governments maintained, Nobel sought consolation in the hope that his explosives might prove to be the "great deterrent" that would end all war.

But he had a doubt; a doubt that many people feel about our modern "great deterrent" now. He knew he could not be certain that, by increasing the slaughter and the devastation caused by war, his explosives would bring armed conflict to an end.

Before most of his generation, he perceived that, historically, war was already long out-of-date; that science and engineering had destroyed the barriers of time and space; that the Arms Race by creating distrust and fear, must obscure the peoples' understanding of where their true interests lay; that War, if it should come, might imperil, or indeed destroy, the great achievements, in literature, in medicine, in science, which our Western civilization had begun to show.

With this magnificent conception of human glory in his mind, he devoted his great fortune to promote the pursuit of knowledge, of beauty, and of wisdom, and which should combat what he thought the deadly foolishness of war.

What a superb example to others of his generation; how tragic that these others did not follow where he led!

Suppose that Krupps, and the Hugenberg Konzern, and the Comité des Forges and others had combined with Nobel to use their power to promote the cause of peace: how different the course of history might have been!

But in Scandinavia, at least, Nobel's victory was complete. I remember, with grateful admiration, how, year by year, Norwegian delegations to the League of Nations, led by Fridtjof Nansen, and with Mr. Hambro, Dr. Christian Lange, Mr. Koht, Dr. Worm-Müller, Ambassador Andvord, Ambassador Skylstad and many other eminent leaders who are gone, came to Geneva to stand with splendid courage for the principles in which Alfred Nobel had believed; how, year by year, their cooperation with the Swedish and the Danish delegations, with Branting and Östen Undén, grew ever closer; how, year by year, the influence of the Scandinavian bloc increased.

If the League of Nations came close to full success, as history will record it did, it owed very much to that cooperation, which Alfred Nobel first inspired.

Now the excitement and the early vision may seem less, but the Scandinavian work still faithfully and persistently goes on; now its doctrines are declared by the leading rulers of the world.

It was President Eisenhower who said that: "Every gun that is made, every warship launched, every rocket fired, signifies, in the final sense, a theft from those who hunger and are not fed, those who are cold and are not clothed. The world in arms is not spending money alone. It is spending the sweat of its labourers, the genius of its scientists, the hopes of its children."

That was the essence of what Alfred Nobel believed three-quarters of a century ago.

Surely we may hope that this grotesque and tragic paradox may be ended soon.

I have been ten years a Minister of the British Crown, in peace and war; I know the heavy forces of inertia which must be moved, to carry even the smallest of reforms. But I still believe in the saving power of human wisdom. And Norway, to its lovers, is not only a land of romance, of mystery and beauty; it is a land of democratic inspiration and of world-wide hope. May there be born in Norway a great new tidal movement of opinion, with perhaps some modern Nobel, which will bear the nations forward to the salvation they so ardently desire.

DAG HAMMARSKJÖLD
1961

INTRODUCTION

Dag Hjalmar Agne Carl Hammarskjöld (July 29, 1905-September 18, 1961) was the youngest of four sons of Agnes (Almquist) Hammarskjöld and Hjalmar Hammarskjöld, prime minister of Sweden, member of the Hague Tribunal, governor of Uppland, chairman of the Board of the Nobel Foundation. In a brief piece written for a radio program in 1953, Dag Hammarskjöld spoke of the influence of his parents: "From generations of soldiers and government officials on my father's side I inherited a belief that no life was more satisfactory than one of selfless service to your country - or humanity. This service required a sacrifice of all personal interests, but likewise the courage to stand up unflinchingly for your convictions. From scholars and clergymen on my mother's side, I inherited a belief that, in the very radical sense of the Gospels, all men were equals as children of God, and should be met and treated by us as our masters in God."

Hammarskjöld has been credited with having coined the term "planned economy". Along with his eldest brother, Bo, who was then undersecretary in the Ministry of Social Welfare, he drafted the legislation which opened the way to the creation of the present, so-called "welfare state. " In the latter part of this period, he drew attention as an international financial negotiator for his part in the discussions with Great Britain on the postwar economic reconstruction of Europe, in his reshaping of the twelve-year-old United States-Swedish trade agreement, in his participation in the talks which organized the Marshall Plan, and in his leadership on the Executive Committee of the Organization for European Economic Cooperation.

PRIZE ACCEPTANCE SPEECH

Acceptance by Rolf Edberg, (At the award ceremony on December 10, 1961, after Mr. Lutuli had accepted his Peace Prize, Swedish Ambassador to Norway Rolf Edberg, representing the Hammarskjöld family, accepted the Peace Prize for 1961 awarded posthumously to Dag Hammarskjöld.) Swedish Ambassador to Norway, on the occasion of the award of the Nobel Peace Prize in Oslo, December 10, 1961

It is with infinite sadness that I have received, at the request of the administrators of the estate of Dag Hammarskjöld, the prize for the year 1961 awarded posthumously to a friend and fellow countryman.

How thankful I should be if I could present to you what he himself would have thought and said, were he standing here today.

Surely he would have seen it as symbolic to be called to this stage - where so much human goodwill has been honoured - along with the South African advocate of nonviolent liberation: two men of different origin and with different starting points, but both striving toward the same goal.

My compatriot was much concerned with the awakening and fermenting continent which was to become his destiny. He once said that the next decade must belong to Africa or to the atom bomb. He firmly believed that the new countries have an important mission to fulfill in the community of nations. He therefore invested all his strength of will, and at the end more than that, to smooth their road toward the future.

Africa was to be the great test for the philosophy he wished to see brought to life through the United Nations.

Time and again he recurred to the indissoluble connection between peace and human rights. Tolerance, protection by law, equal political rights, and equal economic opportunities for all citizens - were prerequisites for a harmonious life within a nation. They also became requirements for such a life among nations.

He would remind us how man once organized himself in families, how families joined together in tribes and villages, and how tribes and villages developed into peoples and nations. But the nation could not be the end of such development. In the Charter of the United Nations he saw a guide to what he called an organized international community.

With an intensity that grew stronger each year, he stressed in his annual reports to the General Assembly that the United Nations had to be shaped into a dynamic instrument in the service of development. In his last report, in a tone of voice penetrating because of its very restraint, he confronted those member states which were clinging to "the time-honored philosophy of sovereign national states in armed competition, of which the most that may be expected is that they achieve a peaceful coexistence"1. This philosophy did not meet the needs of a world of ever increasing interdependence, where nations have at their disposal armaments of hitherto unknown destructive strength. The United Nations must open up ways to more developed forms of international cooperation.

He dated this report August 17 of this year. It now stands as a last testament.

He found the words of the Charter concerning equal rights for all nations, large and small, filled with life and significance. Above all, it was the small nations, and especially the developing countries, which needed the United Nations for their protection and their future. This was why he refused to step down and to throw the organization to the winds when one of the large nations demanded his resignation.

It was impossible to witness that scene at the stormy session of last year's General Assembly without recalling some words that he once wrote about his own father. "A man of firm convictions does not ask, and does not receive, understanding from those with whom he comes into conflict", he wrote about Hjalmar Hammarskjöld. "A mature man is his own judge. In the end, his only firm support is being faithful to his own convictions." How aptly these words applied to himself when he rose unhesitatingly to defend the idea of a truly international body of civil servants or to uphold the principles of the Charter in the Congo operation!

If he felt any uneasiness, then it was because questions dealing with the peace and welfare of peoples were being treated in an overheated atmosphere. And an eyewitness, looking at him sitting there, deeply serious, with the fingers of his right hand against his cheek, as they always were when he was listening intently, might find himself asking this question: What does he represent, that slender man up there behind the green marble desk? A tradition of polished quiet diplomacy doomed to drown in the rising tide of new clamor? Or is he, with his visions of a world community, a herald of the future?

The latter is what we would like to believe. He himself had no doubt about the convincing force of his ideals. He expressed it thus in the last article that he wrote: "Setbacks in trying to realize the ideal do not prove that the ideal is at fault."

Such a conviction must be based on a determined philosophy of life. No one who met him could help noticing that he had a room of quiet within himself. Probably no one was ever able really to reach into that room.

But perhaps we can think that he found something that was essential to himself in the last book that he was engaged in translating, the powerful work *Ich und Du* [I and Thou], in which the Jewish philosopher Martin Buber sets forth his belief that all real living is meeting. He himself believed that there were invisible bridges on which people could meet as human beings above the confines of ideologies, races, and nations.

And perhaps we may dare to see something significant in the obscurity and seeming futility of what happened on that African September night. Scattered about in the debris of the airplane were some books. Among them was *Ich und Du*, with some pages just translated into Swedish. Just before the plane took off on its nocturnal flight, he had left behind with a friend Thomas à Kempis' *Imitation of Christ7*. Tucked in the pages was the oath of office of the Secretary-General:

"I, Dag Hammarskjöld, solemnly swear to exercise in all loyalty, discretion and conscience the functions entrusted to me as Secretary-General of the United Nations, to discharge these functions and regulate my conduct with the interest of the United Nations only in view..."

Had he stood here today, he would, I believe, have had something to say about service as a self-evident duty.

My fellow countryman became a citizen of the world. He was regarded as such by the people from whom he came. But on that cool autumn day of falling leaves when he was brought back to the Uppsala of his youth, he was ours again, he was back home. Shyly he had guarded his inner world, but at that moment the distance disappeared and we felt that he came very close to us.

Therefore, I can speak on behalf of an entire people when I submit our respectful thanks for the honor that has been bestowed today upon our fellow citizen, the greatest honor a man can have. The Peace Prize awarded to Dag Hammarskjöld will constitute a fund which will bear his name and which will be used for a purpose that was close to his heart.

MARTIN LUTHER KING
1964

INTRODUCTION

Martin Luther King, Jr., (January 15, 1929-April 4, 1968) was born Michael Luther King, Jr., but later had his name changed to Martin. His grandfather began the family's long tenure as pastors of the Ebenezer Baptist Church in Atlanta, serving from 1914 to 1931; his father has served from then until the present, and from 1960 until his death Martin Luther acted as co-pastor. Martin Luther attended segregated public schools in Georgia, graduating from high school at the age of fifteen; he received the B. A. degree in 1948 from Morehouse College, a distinguished Negro institution of Atlanta from which both his father and grandfather had been graduated.

In 1957 he was elected president of the Southern Christian Leadership Conference, an organization formed to provide new leadership for the now burgeoning civil rights movement. The ideals for this organization he took from Christianity; its operational techniques from Gandhi. In the eleven-year period between 1957 and 1968, King traveled over six million miles and spoke over twenty-five hundred times, appearing wherever there was injustice, protest, and action; and meanwhile he wrote five books as well as numerous articles. In these years, he led a massive protest in Birmingham, Alabama, that caught the attention of the entire world, providing what he called a coalition of conscience and inspiring his "Letter from a Birmingham Jail", a manifesto of the Negro revolution; he planned the drives in Alabama for the registration of Negroes as voters; he directed the peaceful march on Washington, D.C., of 250,000 people to whom he delivered his address, "I Have a Dream", he conferred with President John F. Kennedy and campaigned for President Lyndon B. Johnson; he was arrested upwards of twenty times and assaulted at least four times; he was awarded five honorary degrees; was named Man of the Year by *Time* magazine in 1963; and became not only the symbolic leader of American blacks but also a world figure.

At the age of thirty-five, Martin Luther King, Jr., was the youngest man to have received the Nobel Peace Prize. When notified of his selection, he announced that he would turn over the prize money of $54,123 to the furtherance of the civil rights movement.

PRIZE ACCEPTANCE SPEECH

Martin Luther King's Acceptance Speech, on the occasion of the award of the Nobel Peace Prize in Oslo, December 10, 1964

Your Majesty, Your Royal Highness, Mr. President, Excellencies, Ladies and Gentlemen:

I accept the Nobel Prize for Peace at a moment when 22 million Negroes of the United States of America are engaged in a creative battle to end the long night of racial injustice. I accept this award on behalf of a civil rights movement which is moving with determination and a majestic scorn for risk and danger to establish a reign of freedom and a rule of justice. I am mindful that only yesterday in Birmingham, Alabama, our children, crying out for brotherhood, were answered with fire hoses, snarling dogs and even death. I am mindful that only yesterday in Philadelphia, Mississippi, young people seeking to secure the right to vote were brutalized and murdered. And only yesterday more than 40 houses of worship in the State of Mississippi alone were bombed or burned because they offered a sanctuary to those who would not accept segregation. I am mindful that debilitating and grinding poverty afflicts my people and chains them to the lowest rung of the economic ladder.

Therefore, I must ask why this prize is awarded to a movement which is beleaguered and committed to unrelenting struggle; to a movement which has not won the very peace and brotherhood which is the essence of the Nobel Prize.

After contemplation, I conclude that this award which I receive on behalf of that movement is a profound recognition that nonviolence is the answer to the crucial political and moral question of our time - - the need for man to overcome oppression and violence without resorting to violence and oppression. Civilization and violence are antithetical concepts. Negroes of the United States, following the people of India, have demonstrated that nonviolence is not sterile passivity, but a powerful moral force which makes for social transformation. Sooner or later all the people of the world will have to discover a way to live together in peace, and thereby transform this pending cosmic elegy into a creative psalm of brotherhood. If this is to be achieved, man must evolve for all human conflict a method which rejects revenge, aggression and retaliation. The foundation of such a method is love.

The tortuous road which has led from Montgomery, Alabama to Oslo bears witness to this truth. This is a road over which millions of Negroes are travelling to find a new sense of dignity. This same road has opened for all Americans a new era of progress and hope. It has led to a new Civil Rights Bill, and it will, I am convinced, be widened and lengthened into a super highway of justice as Negro and white men in increasing numbers create alliances to overcome their common problems.

I accept this award today with an abiding faith in America and an audacious faith in the future of mankind. I refuse to accept despair as the final response to the ambiguities of history. I refuse to accept the idea that the "isness" of man's present nature makes him morally incapable of reaching up for the eternal "oughtness" that forever confronts him. I refuse to accept the idea that man is mere flotsom and jetsom in the river of life, unable to influence the unfolding events which surround him. I refuse to accept the view that mankind is so tragically bound to the starless midnight of racism and war that the bright daybreak of peace and brotherhood can never become a reality.

I refuse to accept the cynical notion that nation after nation must spiral down a militaristic stairway into the hell of thermonuclear destruction. I believe that unarmed truth and unconditional love will have the final word in reality. This is why right temporarily defeated is stronger than evil triumphant. I believe that even amid today's motor bursts and whining bullets, there is still hope for a brighter tomorrow. I believe that wounded justice, lying prostrate on the blood-flowing streets of our nations, can be lifted from this dust of shame to reign supreme among the children of men. I have the audacity to believe that peoples everywhere can have three meals a day for their bodies, education and culture for their minds, and dignity, equality and freedom for their spirits. I believe that what self-centered men have torn down men other-centered can build up. I still believe that one day mankind will bow before the altars of God and be crowned triumphant over war and bloodshed, and nonviolent redemptive good will proclaim the rule of the land. "And the lion and the lamb shall lie down together and every man shall sit under his own vine and fig tree and none shall be afraid." I still believe that We *Shall* overcome!

This faith can give us courage to face the uncertainties of the future. It will give our tired feet new strength as we continue our forward stride toward the city of freedom. When our days become dreary with low-hovering clouds and our nights become darker than a thousand midnights, we will know that we are living in the creative turmoil of a genuine civilization struggling to be born.

Today I come to Oslo as a trustee, inspired and with renewed dedication to humanity. I accept this prize on behalf of all men who love peace and brotherhood. I say I come as a trustee, for in the depths of my heart I am aware that this prize is much more than an honor to me personally.

Every time I take a flight, I am always mindful of the many people who make a successful journey possible - the known pilots and the unknown ground crew.

So you honor the dedicated pilots of our struggle who have sat at the controls as the freedom movement soared into orbit. You honor, once again, Chief Lutuli of South Africa, whose struggles with and for his people, are still met with the most brutal expression of man's inhumanity to man. You honor the ground crew without whose labor and sacrifices the jet flights to freedom could never have left the earth. Most of these people will never make the headline and their names will not appear in *Who's Who*. Yet when years have rolled past and when the blazing light of truth is focused on this marvellous age in which we live - men and women will know and children will be taught that we have a finer land, a better people, a more noble civilization - because these humble children of God were willing to suffer for righteousness' sake.

I think Alfred Nobel would know what I mean when I say that I accept this award in the spirit of a curator of some precious heirloom which he holds in trust for its true owners - all those to whom beauty is truth and truth beauty - and in whose eyes the beauty of genuine brotherhood and peace is more precious than diamonds or silver or gold.

MOTHER TERESA
1979

INTRODUCTION

Mother Teresa, winner of the Nobel Peace Prize, attained world wide fame for her life dedicated to serving the poor and destitute.

Mother Teresa was born (1910) in Akopje, Kosovo in what is now the Republic of Macedonia. Little is known about her early life but at a young age she felt a calling to serve through helping the poor. At the age of 18 she was given permission to join a group of nuns in Ireland. After a few months of training Mother Teresa travelled to Calcutta, India where she formally accepted the vows of a nun.

In her early years she worked as a teacher in the slums of Calcutta, the widespread poverty made a deep impression on her and this led to her starting a new order called "The Missionaries of Charity". Throughout her life Mother Teresa has been given some of the most prestigious awards throughout the Globe.

Mother Teresa was awarded the Nobel Prize "for work undertaken in the struggle to overcome poverty and distress, which also constitute a threat to peace." She refused the conventional ceremonial banquet given to laureates, and asked that the $6,000 funds be given to the poor in Calcutta.

When Mother Teresa received the prize, she was asked, "What can we do to promote world peace?" Her answer was simple: "Go home and love your family ."

Over the last two decades of her life Mother Teresa suffered various health problems but nothing could dissuade her from fulfilling her mission of serving the poor and needy. Until her very last illness she was active in travelling around the world to the different brances of "The Missionaries of Charity"

Mother Teresa suffered a heart attack in Rome in 1983, while visiting Pope John Paul II. After a second attack in 1989, she received an artificial pacemaker. In 1991, after a battle with pneumonia while in Mexico, she suffered further heart problems. She offered to resign her position as head of the Missionaries of Charity. But the nuns of the order, in a secret ballot, voted for her to stay. Mother Teresa agreed to continue her work as head of the order.

In April 1996, Mother Teresa fell and broke her collar bone. In August she suffered from malaria and failure of the left heart ventricle. She had heart surgery, but it was clear that her health was declining. On March 13, 1997, she stepped down from the head of Missionaries of Charity and died on September 5, 1997, nine days after her 87th birthday.

Mother Teresa was a living saint who offered a great example and inspiration to the world.

PRIZE ACCEPTANCE SPEECH

Oslo, Norway, 11 December 1979

As we have gathered here together to thank God for the Nobel Peace Prize, I think it will be beautiful that we pray the prayer of St. Francis of Assisi which always surprises me very much . We pray this prayer every day after Holy Communion, because it is very fitting for each one of us.

And I always wonder that 400-500 years ago when St. Francis of Assisi composed this prayer, they had the same difficulties that we have today as we compose this prayer that fits very nicely for us also. I think some of you already have got it - so we pray together: Let us thank God for the opportunity that we all have together today, for this gift of peace that reminds us that we have been created to live that peace, and that Jesus became man to bring that good news to the poor.

He, being God, became man in all things like us except in sin, and he proclaimed very clearly that he had come to give the good news. The news was peace to all of good will and this is something that we all want - the peace of heart. And God loved the world so much that he gave his son - it was a giving: it is as much as if to say it hurt God to give, because he loved the world so much that he gave his son. He gave him to the Virgin Mary, and what did she do with him?

As soon as he came in her life, immediately she went in haste to give that good news, and as she came into the house of her cousin, the child - the child in the womb of Elizabeth, lept with joy. He was, that little unborn child was, the first messenger of peace. He recognized the Prince of Peace, he recognized that Christ had come to bring the good news for you and for me.

And as if that was not enough - it was not enough to become a man - he died on the cross to show that greater love, and he died for you and for me and for that leper and for that man dying of hunger and that naked person lying in the street not only of Calcutta, but of Africa, and New York, and London, and Oslo - and insisted that we love one another as he loves each one of us.

And we read that in the Gospel very clearly: "love as I have loved you; as I love you; as the Father has loved me, I love you." And the harder the Father loved him, he gave him to us, and how much we love one another, we too must give to each other until it hurts. It is not enough for us to say: "I love God, but I do not love my neighbor." Saint John says that you are a liar if you say you love God and you don't love your neighbor.

How can you love God whom you do not see, if you do not love your neighbor whom you see, whom you touch, with whom you live? And so this is very important for us to realize that love, to be true, has to hurt. It hurt Jesus to love us. It hurt him. And to make sure we remember his great love, he made himself the bread of life to satisfy our hunger for his love - our hunger for God - because we have been created for that love. We have been created in his image.

We have been created to love and to be loved, and he has become man to make it possible for us to love as he loved us. He makes himself the hungry one, the naked one, the homeless one, and he says: " You did it to me". he is hungry for our love, and this is the hunger that you and I must find. It may be in our own home. I never forget an opportunity I had in visiting a home where they had all these old parents of sons and daughters who had just put them in an institution and forgotten, maybe.

And I went there, and I saw in that home they had everything, beautiful things, but everybody was looking towards the door. And I did not see a singe one with a smile on their face. And I turned to the sister and I asked: How is that? How is that these people who have everything here, why are they all looking towards the door? Why are they not smiling? I am so used to see the smiles on our people, even the dying ones smile. And she said: "This is nearly every day.

They are expecting, they are hoping that a son or daughter will come to visit them. They are hurt because they are forgotten." And see - this is where love comes. That poverty comes right there in our own home, even neglect to love. Maybe in our own family we have somebody who is feeling lonely, who is feeling sick, who is feeling worried, and there are difficult days for everybody. Are we there?

Are we there to Receive them? Is the mother there to receive the child? I was surprised in the West to see so many young boys and girls given into drugs. And I tried to find out why. Why is it like that? And the answer was: "Because there is no one in the family to receive them." Father and mother are so busy they have no time. Young parents are in some institution and the child goes back to the street and gets involved in something.

We are talking of peace. These are things that break peace. But I feel the greatest destroyer of peace today is abortion, because it is a direct war, a direct killing, direct murder by the mother herself. And we read in the scripture, for God says very clearly: "Even if a mother could forget her child, I will not forget you. I have curved you in the palm of my hand." We are curved in the palm of his hand; so close to him, that unborn child has been curved in the hand of God.

And that is what strikes me most, the beginning of that sentence, that even if a mother could forget, something impossible - but even if she could forget - I will not forget you. And today the greatest means, the greatest destroyer of peace is abortion. And we who are standing here - our parents wanted us. We would not be here if our parents would do that to us. Our children, we want them, we love them.

But what of the other millions. Many people are very, very

concerned with the children of India, with the children of Africa where quite a number die, maybe of malnutrition, of hunger and so on, but millions are dying deliberately by the will of the mother. And this is what is the greatest destroyer of peace today. Because if a mother can kill her own child, what is left for me to kill you and you to kill me? There is nothing between. And this I appeal in India, I appeal everywhere - "Let us bring the child back" - and this year being the child's year: What have we done for the child?

At the beginning of the year I told, I spoke everywhere and I said: let us ensure this year that we make every single child born, and unborn, wanted. And today is the end of the year. Have we really made the children wanted? I will tell you something terrifying. We are fighting abortion by adoption. We have saved thousands of lives. We have sent word to all the clinics, to the hospitals, police stations: "Please don't destroy the child; we will take the child".

So every hour of the day and night there is always somebody - we have quite a number of unwedded mothers - tell them: "Come, we will take care of you, we will take care of the child from you, and we will get a home for the child". And we have a tremendous demand for families who have no children, that is the blessing of God for us. And also, we are doing another thing which is very beautiful. We are teaching our beggars, our leprosy patients, our slum dwellers, our people of the street, natural family planning.

And in Calcutta alone in six years - it is all in Calcutta - we have had 61 273 babies less from the families who would have had them because they practice this natural way of abstaining, of self-control, out of love for each other. We teach them the temperature method which is very beautiful, very simple. And our poor people understand. And you know what they have told me? "Our family is healthy, our family is united, and we can have a baby whenever we want".

So clear - those people in the street, those beggars - and I think that if our people can do like that how much more you and all the others who can know the ways and means without destroying the life that God has created in us. The poor people are very great people. They can teach us so many beautiful things. The other day one of them came to thank us and said: "You people who have evolved chastity; you are the best people to teach us family planning because it is nothing more than self-control out of love for each other."

And I think they said a beautiful sentence. And these are people who maybe have nothing to eat, maybe they have not a home where to live, but they are great people. The poor are very wonderful people. One evening we went out and we picked up four people from the street. And one of them was in a most terrible condition. And I told the sisters: "You take care of the other three; I will take care of this one that looks worse." So I did for her all that my love can do. I put her in bed, and there was such a beautiful smile on her face.

She took hold of my hand, as she said one word only: "thank you" - and she died. I could not help but examine my conscience before her. And I asked: "What would I say if I was in her place?" And my answer was very simple. I would have tried to draw a little attention to myself. I would have said: "I am hungry, I am dying, I am cold, I am in pain", or something. But she gave me much more - she gave me her grateful love.

And she died with a smile on her face - like that man who we picked up from the drain, half eaten with worms, and we brought him to the home - "I have lived like an animal in the street, but I am going to die like an angel, loved and cared for." And it was so wonderful to see the greatness of that man who could speak like that, who could die like that without blaming, without cursing anybody, without comparing anything. Like an angel - this is the greatness of our people.

And this is why we believe what Jesus has said: "I was hungry; I was naked, I was homeless; I was unwanted, unloved, uncared for - and you did it to me." I believe that we are not really social workers. We may be doing social work in the eyes of people. But we are really contemplatives in the heart of the world. For we are touching the body of Christ twenty-four hours. We have twenty-four hours in his presence, and so you and I. You too must try to bring that presence of God into your family, for the family that prays together stays together.

And I think that we in our family, we don't need bombs and guns, to destroy or to bring peace - just get together, love one another, bring that peace, that joy, that strength of presence of each other in the home. And we will be able to overcome all the evil that is in the world. There is so much suffering, so much hatred, so much misery, and we with our prayer, with our sacrifice are beginning at home. Love begins at home, and it is not how much we do, but how much love we put in the action that we do.

It is to God almighty - how much we do does not matter, because he is infinite, but how much love we put in action. How much we do to him in the person that we are serving. Some time ago in Calcutta we had great difficulty in getting sugar. And I don't know how the word got around to the children, and a little boy of four years old, a Hindu boy, went home and told his parents: "I will not eat sugar for three days.

I will give my sugar to Mother Teresa for her children." After these three days his father and mother brought him to our house. I had never met them before, and this little one could scarcely pronounce my name. But he knew exactly what he had come to do. He knew that he wanted to share his love. And this is why I have received such a lot of love from all. From the time that I have come here I have simply been surrounded with love, and with real, real understanding love.

It could feel as if everyone in India, everyone in Africa is somebody very special for to you. And I felt quite home, I was telling Sister today. If feel in the convent with the Sisters as if I am in Calcutta with my own Sisters. So completely at home here, right here. And so here I am talking with you. I want you to find the poor here, right in your own home first. And begin love there. Be that good news to your own people. And find out about your next-door neighbor.

Do you know who they are? I had the most extraordinary experience with a Hindu family who had eight children. A gentleman came to our house and said: "Mother Teresa, there is a family with eight children; they have not eaten for so long; do something". So I took some rice and I went there immediately. And I saw the children - their eyes shining with hunger. I don't know if you have ever seen hunger. But I have seen it very often.

And she took the rice, she divided the rice, and she went out. When she came back I asked her: "Where did you go, what did you do?" And she gave me a very simple answer: "They are hungry also". What struck me most was that she knew - and who are they? a Muslim family - and she knew. I didn't bring more rice that evening because I wanted them to enjoy the joy of sharing. But there were those children radiating joy, sharing the joy with their mother because she had the love to give.

And you see this is where love begins - at home. And I want you - and I am very grateful for what I have received. It has been a tremendous experience and I go back to India - I will be back by next week, the 15th I hope, and I will be able to bring your love. And I know well that you have not given from your abundance, but you have given until it has hurt you. Today the little children, they gave - I was so surprised - there is so much joy for the children that are hungry.

That the children like themselves will need love and get so much from their parents. So let us thank God that we have had this opportunity to come to know each other, and that this knowledge of each other has brought us very close. And we will be able to help the children of the whole world, because as you know our Sisters are all over the world. And with this prize that I have received as a prize of peace, I am going to try to make the home for many people that have no home.

Because I believe that love begins at home, and if we can create a home for the poor, I think that more and more love will spread. And we will be able through this understanding love to bring peace, be the good news to the poor. The poor in our own family first, in our country and in the world. To be able to do this, our Sisters, our lives have to be woven with prayer. They have to be woven with Christ to be able to understand, to be able to share. Today, there is so much suffering and I feel that the passion of Christ is being relived all over again.

Are we there to share that passion, to share that suffering of people - around the world, not only the poor countries. But I found the poverty of the West so much more difficult to remove. When I pick up a person from the street, hungry, I give him a plate of rice, a piece of bread, I have satisfied. I have removed that hunger. But a person that is shut out, that feels unwanted, unloved, terrified, the person that has been thrown out from society - that poverty is so hurtful and so much, and I find that very difficult.

Our Sisters are working amongst that kind of people in the West. So you must pray for us that we may be able to be that good news. We cannot do that without you. You have to do that here in your country. You must come to know the poor. Maybe our people her have material things, everything, but I think that if we all look into our own homes, how difficult we find it sometimes to smile at each other, and that the smile is the beginning of love.

And so let us always meet each other with a smile, for the smile is the beginning of love, and once we begin to love each other, naturally we want to do something. So you pray for our Sisters and for me and for our Brothers, and for our Co-Workers that are around the world. Pray that we may remain faithful to the gift of God, to love him and serve him in the poor together with you.

What we have done we would not have been able to do if you did not share with your prayers, with your gifts, this continual giving. But I don't want you to give me from your abundance. I want you to give me until it hurts. The other day I received $15 from a man who has been on his back for twenty years and the only part that he can move is his right hand. And the only companion that he enjoys is smoking. And he said to me: "I do not smoke for one week, and I send you this money." It must have been a terrible sacrifice for him but see how beautiful, how he shared. And with that money I brought bread and I gave to those who are hungry with a joy on both sides. He was giving and the poor were receiving.

This is something you and I can do - it is a gift of God to us to be able to share our love with others. And let it be able to share our love with others. And let it be as it was for Jesus. Let us love one another as he loved us. Let us love him with undivided love. And the joy of loving him and each other - let us give now that Christmas is coming so close. Let us keep that joy of loving Jesus in our hearts, and share that joy with all that we come in touch with.

That radiating joy with all that we come in touch with. That radiating joy is real, for we have no reason not to be happy because we have Christ with us. Christ in our hearts, Christ in the poor that we meet, Christ in the smile that we give and the smile that we receive. Let us make that one point - that no child will be unwanted and also that we meet each other always with a smile, especially when it is difficult to smile.

I never forget some time ago about fourteen professors came from the United States from different universities. And they came to Calcutta to our house. Then we were talking about the fact that they had been to the home for the dying. (We have a home for the dying in Calcutta, where we have picked up more than 36 000 people only from the streets of and out of that big number more than 18 000 have died a beautiful death. They have just gone home to God). And they came to our house and we talked of love, of compassion.

And then one of them asked me: "Say, Mother, please tell us something that we will remember". And I said to them: 'Smile at each other, make time for each other in your family. Smile at each other." And then another one asked me: "Are you married?" and I said: "Yes, and I find it sometimes very difficult to smile at Jesus because he can be very demanding sometimes". This is really something true. And there is where love comes - when it is demanding, and yet we can give it to him with joy.

Just as I have said today, I have said that if I don't go to heaven for anything else I will be going to heaven for all the publicity because it has purified me and sacrificed me and made me really ready to go to heaven. I think that this is something, that we must live life beautifully, we have Jesus with us and he loves us. If we could only remember that God loves us, and we have an opportunity to love others as he loves us, not in big things, but i small things with great love, then Norway becomes a nest of love.

And how beautiful it will be that from here a center for peace from war has been given. That from here the joy of life of the unborn child comes out. If you become a burning light of peace in the world, then really the Nobel Peace Prize is a gift of the Norwegian people.

God bless you! You will get credit for it.

THE 14TH DALAI LAMA
1989

INTRODUCTION

His Holiness the XIVth Dalai Lama, Tenzin Gyatso, is the spiritual and temporal leader of the Tibetan people. He was born in a small village called Takster in north eastern Tibet. He began his education at the age of six and completed the Geshe Lharampa Degree (Doctorate of Buddhist Philosophy) when he was 25.

In 1950, at 16, His Holiness was called upon to assume full political power as Head of State and Government when Tibet was threatened by the might of China. In 1954 he went to Peking to talk with Mao Tse-Tung and other Chinese leaders, including Chou En-Lai and Deng Xiaoping. In 1956, while visiting India to attend the 2500th Buddha Jayanti, he had a series of meetings with Prime Minister Nehru and Premier Chou about deteriorating conditions in Tibet. In 1959 he was forced into exile in India after the Chinese military occupation of Tibet. Since 1960 he has resided in Dharamsala, aptly known as "Little Lhasa", the seat of the Tibetan Government-in-Exile.

His Holiness continues to present new initiatives to resolve the Tibetan issues. At the Congressional Human Rights Caucus in 1987 he proposed a Five-Point Peace Plan as a first step towards resolving the future status of Tibet.

Unlike his predecessors, His Holiness has met and talked with many Westerners and has visited the United States, Canada, Western Europe, the United Kingdom, the Soviet Union, Mongolia, Greece, Japan, Thailand, Malaysia, Singapore,

Indonesia, Nepal, Costa Rica, Mexico, the Vatican, China and Australia. He has met with religious leaders from all these countries.

His Holiness met with the late Pope Paul VI at the Vatican in 1973, and with His Holiness Pope John Paul II in 1980, 1982, 1986 and 1988.

Since his first visit to the west in the early 1970s, His Holiness' reputation as a scholar and man of peace has grown steadily. In recent years, a number of western universities and institutions have conferred Peace Awards and honorary Doctorate Degrees upon His Holiness in recognition of his distinguished writings in Buddhist philosophy and of his distinguished leadership in the service of freedom and peace.

PRIZE ACCEPTANCE SPEECH

The 14th Dalai Lama's Acceptance Speech, on the occasion of the award of the Nobel Peace Prize in Oslo, December 10, 1989

Your Majesty, Members of the Nobel Committee, Brothers and Sisters:

I am very happy to be here with you today to receive the Nobel Prize for Peace. I feel honoured, humbled and deeply moved that you should give this important prize to a simple monk from Tibet. I am no one special. But, I believe the prize is a recognition of the true values of altruism, love, compassion and nonviolence which I try to practise, in accordance with the teachings of the Buddha and the great sages of India and Tibet.

I accept the prize with profound gratitude on behalf of the oppressed everywhere and for all those who struggle for freedom and work for world peace. I accept it as a tribute to the man who founded the modern tradition of nonviolent action for change - Mahatma Gandhi - whose life taught and inspired me. And, of course, I accept it on behalf of the six million Tibetan people, my brave countrymen and women inside Tibet, who have suffered and continue to suffer so much. They confront a calculated and systematic strategy aimed at the destruction of their national and cultural identities. The prize reaffirms our conviction that with truth, courage and determination as our weapons, Tibet will be liberated.

No matter what part of the world we come from, we are all basically the same human beings. We all seek happiness and try to avoid suffering. We have the same basic human needs and concerns. All of us human beings want freedom and the right to determine our own destiny as individuals and as peoples. That is human nature. The great changes that are taking place everywhere in the world, from Eastern Europe to Africa, are a clear indication of this.

In China the popular movement for democracy was crushed by brutal force in June this year. But I do not believe the demonstrations were in vain, because the spirit of freedom was rekindled among the Chinese people and China cannot escape the impact of this spirit of freedom sweeping many parts of the world. The brave students and their supporters showed the Chinese leadership and the world the human face of that great nation.

Last week a number of Tibetans were once again sentenced to prison terms of up to nineteen years at a mass show trial, possibly intended to frighten the population before today's event. Their only "crime" was the expression of the widespread desire of Tibetans for the restoration of their beloved country's independence.

The suffering of our people during the past forty years of occupation is well documented. Ours has been a long struggle. We know our cause is just. Because violence can only breed more violence and suffering, our struggle must remain nonviolent and free of hatred. We are trying to end the suffering of our people, not to inflict suffering upon others.

It is with this in mind that I proposed negotiations between Tibet and China on numerous occasions. In 1987, I made specific proposals in a five-point plan for the restoration of peace and human rights in Tibet. This included the conversion of the entire Tibetan plateau into a Zone of Ahimsa, a sanctuary of peace and nonviolence where human beings and nature can live in peace and harmony.

Last year, I elaborated on that plan in Strasbourg, at the European Parliament. I believe the ideas I expressed on those occasions are both realistic and reasonable, although they have been criticised by some of my people as being too conciliatory. Unfortunately, China's leaders have not responded positively to the suggestions we have made, which included important concessions. If this continues we will be compelled to reconsider our position.

Any relationship between Tibet and China will have to be based on the principle of equality, respect, trust and mutual benefit. It will also have to be based on the principle which the wise rulers of Tibet and of China laid down in a treaty as early as 823 A.D., carved on the pillar which still stands today in front of the Jo-khang, Tibet's holiest shrine, in Lhasa, that "Tibetans will live happily in the great land of Tibet, and the Chinese will live happily in the great land of China".

As a Buddhist monk, my concern extends to all members of the human family and, indeed, to all sentient beings who suffer. I believe all suffering is caused by ignorance. People inflict pain on others in the selfish pursuit of their happiness or satisfaction. Yet true happiness comes from a sense of inner peace and contentment, which in turn must be achieved through the cultivation of altruism, of love and compassion and elimination of ignorance, selfishness and greed.

The problems we face today, violent conflicts, destruction of nature, poverty, hunger, and so on, are human-created problems which can be resolved through human effort, understanding and the development of a sense of brotherhood and sisterhood. We need to cultivate a universal responsibility for one another and the planet we share. Although I have found my own Buddhist religion helpful in generating love and compassion, even for those we consider our enemies, I am convinced that everyone can develop a good heart and a sense of universal responsibility with or without religion.

With the ever-growing impact of science on our lives, religion and spirituality have a greater role to play by reminding us of our humanity. There is no contradiction between the two. Each gives us valuable insights into the other. Both science and the teachings of the Buddha tell us of the fundamental unity of all things. This understanding is crucial if we are to take positive and decisive action on the pressing global concern with the environment. I believe all religions pursue the same goals, that of cultivating human goodness and bringing happiness to all human beings. Though the means might appear different the ends are the same. As we enter the final decade of this century I am optimistic that the ancient values that have sustained mankind are today reaffirming themselves to prepare us for a kinder, happier twenty-first century. I pray for all of us, oppressor and friend, that together we succeed in building a better world through human understanding and love, and that in doing so we may reduce the pain and suffering of all sentient beings.

Thank you.

MIKHAIL GORBACHEV
1990

INTRODUCTION

Gorbachev, Mikhail Se1rgeyevich, 2 March, 1931–, Soviet political leader. Born in the agricultural region of Stavropol, Gorbachev studied law at Moscow Univ., where in 1953 he married a philosophy student, Raisa Maksimovna Titorenko (1932?–99). Returning to Stavropol, he moved gradually upward in the local Communist party. In 1970, he became Stavropol party leader and was elected to the Supreme Soviet of the USSR. Regarded as a skilled technocrat and a reformer, Gorbachev joined (1978) the Communist party secretariat as agriculture secretary, and in 1980 he joined the politburo as the protégé of Yuri Andropov. After Andropov's ascension to party leadership, Gorbachev assumed (1983) full responsibility for the economy.

Following the death of Konstantin Chernenko (Andropov's successor) in 1985, Gorbachev was appointed general secretary of the party despite being the youngest member of the politburo. The nuclear disaster at Chernobyl (1986) forced Gorbachev to allow even greater freedom of expression. The government released political prisoners, allowed increased emigration, attacked corruption, and encouraged the critical reexamination of Soviet history.

In a series of summit talks (1985–88), Gorbachev improved relations with U.S. President Ronald Reagan, with whom he signed an Intermediate Nuclear Forces (INF) arms limitation treaty in 1987. By 1989 he had brought about the end of the

Soviet occupation of Afghanistan and had sanctioned the end of the Communist monopoly on political power in Eastern Europe. For his contributions to reducing East-West tensions, he was awarded the 1990 Nobel Peace Prize. By 1990, however, Gorbachev's *perestroika* program had failed to deliver significant improvement in the economy, and the elimination of political and social control had released latent ethnic and national tensions in the Baltic states, in the constituent republics of Armenia, Georgia, Ukraine, and Moldova, and elsewhere.

Gorbachev dissolved the Communist party, granted the Baltic states independence, and proposed a much looser, chiefly economic federation among the remaining republics. With the formation of the Commonwealth of Independent States (CIS) on Dec. 8, 1991, the federal government of the Soviet Union became superfluous, and on Dec. 25, Gorbachev resigned as president. Since 1992, Gorbachev has headed international organizations; written several books, including *On My Country and the World* (tr. 1999), and run unsuccessfully (1996) for the Russian presidency.

PRIZE ACCEPTANCE SPEECH

(Read by Andrej Kovaljov.)

As the Laureate was unable to be present on the occasion of the award of the Nobel Peace Prize in Oslo, December 10, 1990, the acceptance was read by Andrej Kovaljov.

(Translation)

Your Majesty, Esteemed Chairman of the Norwegian Nobel Committee, Ladies and gentlemen,

I have been requested by the President of the USSR, Mikhail Gorbachev, to present his address to the Norwegian Nobel Committee and to all those present today at this award ceremony:

To the Chairman of the Norwegian Nobel Committee, Mrs. Gidske Anderson: Esteemed Mrs. Anderson, I am deeply and personally moved by the decision of the Nobel Committee to award me the 1990 Nobel Peace Prize.

The prestige and authority of the Nobel Peace Prize are universally recognised. The prize has been awarded ever since the beginning of this century. The disasters and tragedies of this period, which have not managed to subdue man's optimism and unflagging belief in human reason, have given the Peace Prize the unique aura associated with it today.

Immanuel Kant prophesied that mankind would one day be faced with a dilemma: either to be joined in a true union of nations or to perish in a war of annihilation ending in the extinction of the human race.' Now, as we move from the second to the third millennium, the clock has struck the moment of truth.

In this respect, the year 1990 represents a turning point. It marks the end of the unnatural division of Europe. Germany has been reunited. We have begun resolutely to tear down the material foundations of a military, political and ideological confrontation. But there are some very grave threats that have not been eliminated: the potential for conflict and the primitive instincts which allow it, aggressive intentions, and totalitarian traditions.

I would like to assure you that the leadership of the USSR is doing and will continue to do everything in its power to ensure that future developments in Europe and the world as a whole are based on openness, mutual trust, international law and universal values.

The recent meeting in Paris of heads of state and government from the European nations, the United States and Canada, embodying all the best elements in international movements such as the Helsinki Process, has established the framework for a Europe based on the rule of law, stability, good relations between neighbouring countries and humane attitudes.' It is my hope that such a Europe will be understood and accepted by nations and governments in other parts of the world as an example of universal security and genuine cooperation.

I do not regard the 1990 Nobel Peace Prize as an award to me personally, but as a recognition of what we call perestroika and innovative political thinking, which is of vital significance for human destinies all over the world.

The Nobel Peace Prize for 1990 confirms that perestroika and innovative political thinking no longer belong only to us, the people of the Soviet Union. They are the property of the whole of mankind and are an inseparable part of its destiny and of a safe, peaceful future. We are deeply grateful to Norway and other members of the international community who have shown such understanding and who, through their conduct in international issues and in their relations with the Soviet Union, have shown their solidarity as we proceed with our perestroika and their sympathy as we struggle to resolve our problems. If we all took this as our point of departure, mankind would have no cause to regret the loss of a unique opportunity for reason and the logic of peace to prevail over that of war and alienation.

Once more, I would like to express my appreciation for this very great honour. I intend to do everything in my power to live up to the expectations and hopes of my countrymen and all those who support the Nobel Committee's choice.

With my sincere wishes for peace and prosperity,

Mikhail Gorbachev

President of the USSR

This was the address by the winner of the Nobel Peace Prize for 1990, which I, as his personal representative, have had the honour of making on his behalf.

Thank you for your attention.

AUNG SAN SUU KYI
1991

INTRODUCTION

Aung San Suu Kyi , 1945–, Burmese political leader. The daughter of assassinated (1947) nationalist general U Aung San, who is regarded as the founder of modern Myanmar, she lived outside the country after 1960. Returning in 1988 to care for her dying mother, she joined the opposition to U Ne Win and became leader of the National League for Democracy (NLD).

Her outspoken criticism of the military leaders of Myanmar and the memory of her father made her a symbol of popular desire for political freedom and a focus of opposition to the dictatorship.

In July, 1989, she was placed under house arrest. The NLD won 80% of the seats in 1990 elections for parliament, but the military refused to yield power.

Awarded the 1990 Sakharov Prize from the European Parliament and the 1991 Nobel Peace Prize for her nonviolent struggle, she remained under house arrest until 1995 and was subsequently subject to severe restrictions.

Nonetheless, she has stayed in Myanmar, continuing to write and speak for her cause. She subsequently has been placed in house arrest or detention from Sept., 2000, to May, 2002, and since May, 2003.

PRIZE ACCEPTANCE SPEECH

Acceptance Speech delivered on behalf of Aung San Suu Kyi, by her son Alexander Aris, on the occasion of the award of the Nobel Peace Prize in Oslo, December 10, 1991

Your Majesties, Your Excellencies, Ladies and Gentlemen, I stand before you here today to accept on behalf of my mother, Aung San Suu Kyi, this greatest of prizes, the Nobel Prize for Peace. Because circumstances do not permit my mother to be here in person, I will do my best to convey the sentiments I believe she would express.

Firstly, I know that she would begin by saying that she accepts the Nobel Prize for Peace not in her own name but in the name of all the people of Burma. She would say that this prize belongs not to her but to all those men, women and children who, even as I speak, continue to sacrifice their wellbeing, their freedom and their lives in pursuit of a democratic Burma. Theirs is the prize and theirs will be the eventual victory in Burma's long struggle for peace, freedom and democracy.

Speaking as her son, however, I would add that I personally believe that by her own dedication and personal sacrifice she has come to be a worthy symbol through whom the plight of all the people of Burma may be recognised. And no one must underestimate that plight. The plight of those in the countryside and towns, living in poverty and destitution, those in prison, battered and tortured; the plight of the young people, the hope of Burma, dying of malaria in the jungles to which they have fled; that of the Buddhist monks, beaten and dishonoured. Nor should we forget the many senior and highly respected leaders besides my mother who are all incarcerated. It is on their behalf that I thank you, from my heart, for this supreme honour. The Burmese people can today hold their heads a little higher in the knowledge that in this far distant land their suffering has been heard and heeded.

We must also remember that the lonely struggle taking place in a heavily guarded compound in Rangoon is part of the much larger struggle, worldwide, for the emancipation of the human spirit from political tyranny and psychological subjection. The Prize, I feel sure, is also intended to honour all those engaged in this struggle wherever they may be. It is not without reason that today's events in Oslo fall on the International Human Rights Day, celebrated throughout the world. 1

Mr. Chairman, the whole international community has applauded the choice of your committee. Just a few days ago, the United Nations passed a unanimous and historic resolution welcoming Secretary-General Javier Pérez de Cuéllar's statement on the significance of this award and endorsing his repeated appeals for my mother's early release from detention. Universal concern at the grave human rights situation in Burma was clearly expressed. Alone and isolated among the entire nations of the world a single dissenting voice was heard, from the military junta in Rangoon, too late and too weak.

This regime has through almost thirty years of misrule reduced the once prosperous 'Golden Land' of Burma to one of the world's most economically destitute nations. In their heart of hearts even those in power now in Rangoon must know that their eventual fate will be that of all totalitarian regimes who seek to impose their authority through fear, repression and hatred. When the present Burmese struggle for democracy erupted onto the streets in 1988, it was the first of what became an international tidal wave of such movements throughout Eastern Europe, Asia and Africa. Today, in 1991, Burma stands conspicuous in its continued suffering at the hands of a repressive, intransigent junta, the State Law and Order Restoration Council. However, the example of those nations which have successfully achieved democracy holds out an important message to the Burmese people; that, in the last resort, through the sheer economic unworkability of totalitarianism this present regime will be swept away. And today in the face of rising inflation, a mismanaged economy and near worthless Kyat, the Burmese government is undoubtedly reaping as it has sown.

However, it is my deepest hope that it will not be in the face of complete economic collapse that the regime will fall, but that the ruling junta may yet heed such appeals to basic humanity as that which the Nobel Committee has expressed in its award of this year's prize. I know that within the military government there are those to whom the present policies of fear and repression are abhorrent, violating as they do the most sacred principles of Burma's Buddhist heritage. This is no empty wishful thinking but a conviction my mother reached in the course of her dealings with those in positions of authority, illustrated by the election victories of her party in constituencies comprised almost exclusively of military personnel and their families. It is my profoundest wish that these elements for moderation and reconciliation among those now in authority may make their sentiments felt in Burma's hour of deepest need.

I know that if she were free today my mother would, in thanking you, also ask you to pray that the oppressors and the oppressed should throw down their weapons and join together to build a nation founded on humanity in the spirit of peace.

Although my mother is often described as a political dissident who strives by peaceful means for democratic change, we should remember that her quest is basically spiritual. As she has said, "The quintessential revolution is that of the spirit", and she has written of the "essential spiritual aims" of the struggle. The realisation of this depends solely on human responsibility. At the root of that responsibility lies, and I quote, "the concept of perfection, the urge to achieve it, the intelligence to find a path towards it, and the will to follow that path if not to the end, at least the distance needed to rise above individual limitation... ". "To live the full life," she says, "one must have the courage to bear the responsibility of the needs of others ... one must want to bear this responsibility." And she links this firmly to her faith when she writes, "...Buddhism, the foundation of traditional Burmese culture, places the greatest value on man, who alone of all beings can achieve the supreme state of Buddhahood. Each man has in him the potential to realize the truth through his own will and endeavour and to help others to realize it." Finally she says, "The quest for democracy in Burma is the struggle of a people to live whole, meaningful lives as free and equal members of the world community. It is part of the unceasing human endeavour to prove that the spirit of man can transcends the flaws of his nature."2

This is the second time that my younger brother and I have accepted a great prize for my mother in Norway. Last year we travelled to Bergen to receive for her the Thorolf Rafto Prize for Human Rights, a wonderful prelude to this year's event.3 By now we have a very special feeling for the people of Norway. It is my hope that soon my mother will be able to share this feeling and to speak directly for herself instead of through me. Meanwhile this tremendous support for her and the people of Burma has served to bring together two peoples from opposite ends of the earth. I believe much will follow from the links now forged.

It only remains for me to thank you all from the bottom of my heart. Let us hope and pray that from today the wounds start to heal and that in the years to come the 1991 Nobel Prize for Peace will be seen as a historic step towards the achievement of true peace in Burma. The lessons of the past will not be forgotten, but it is our hope for the future that we celebrate today.

NELSON MANDELA
1993

INTRODUCTION

Nelson Rolihlahla Mandela was born in Transkei, South Africa on July 18, 1918. His father was Chief Henry Mandela of the Tembu Tribe. Mandela himself was educated at University College of Fort Hare and the University of Witwatersrand and qualified in law in 1942. He joined the African National Congress in 1944 and was engaged in resistance against the ruling National Party's apartheid policies after 1948. He went on trial for treason in 1956-1961 and was aquitted in 1961.

Mandela was arrested in 1962 and sentenced to five years' imprisonment with hard labour. In 1963, when many fellow leaders of the ANC and the Umkhonto we Sizwe were arrested, Mandela was brought to stand trial with them for plotting to overthrow the government by violence. His statement from the dock received considerable international publicity. On June 12, 1964, eight of the accused, including Mandela, were sentenced to life imprisonment. From 1964 to 1982, he was incarcerated at Robben Island Prison, off Cape Town; thereafter, he was at Pollsmoor Prison, nearby on the mainland.

During his years in prison, Nelson Mandela's reputation grew steadily. He was widely accepted as the most significant black leader in South Africa and became a potent symbol of resistance as the anti-apartheid movement gathered strength. He consistently refused to compromise his political position to obtain his freedom.

Nelson Mandela was released on February 18, 1990. After his release, he plunged himself wholeheartedly into his life's work, striving to attain the goals he and others had set out almost four decades earlier. In 1991, at the first national conference of the ANC held inside South Africa after the organization had been banned in 1960, Mandela was elected President of the ANC while his lifelong friend and colleague, Oliver Tambo, became the organisation's National Chairperson.

PRIZE ACCEPTANCE SPEECH

Acceptance speech of the president of the African National Congress, Nelson Mandela, at the Nobel Peace Prize Award Ceremony.

Oslo, Norway, 10 December 1993

Your Majesty the King,

Your Royal Highness,

Honourable Prime Minister,

Madame Gro Brundtland,

Ministers,

Members of Parliament and Ambassadors,

Esteemed Members of the Norwegian Nobel Committee,

Fellow Laureate, Mr. F.W. de Klerk,

Distinguished guests,

Friends, ladies and gentlemen:

I am indeed truly humbled to be standing here today to receive this year's Nobel Peace Prize.

I extend my heartfelt thanks to the Norwegian Nobel Committee for elevating us to the status of a Nobel Peace Prize winner.

I would also like to take this opportunity to congratulate my compatriot and fellow laureate, State President F.W. de Klerk, on his receipt of this high honour.

Together, we join two distinguished South Africans, the late Chief Albert Luthuli and His Grace Archbishop Desmond Tutu, to whose seminal contributions to the peaceful struggle against the evil system of apartheid you paid well-deserved tribute by awarding them the Nobel Peace Prize.

It will not be presumptuous of us if we also add, among our predecessors, the name of another outstanding Nobel Peace Prize winner, the late African- American statesman and internationalist, the Rev Martin Luther King Jr.

He, too, grappled with and died in the effort to make a contribution to the just solution of the same great issues of the day which we have had to face as South Africans.

We speak here of the challenge of the dichotomies of war and peace, violence and non-violence, racism and human dignity, oppression and repression and liberty and human rights, poverty and freedom from want.

We stand here today as nothing more than a representative of the millions of our people who dared to rise up against a social system whose very essence is war, violence, racism, oppression, repression and the impoverishment of an entire people.

I am also here today as a representative of the millions of people across the globe, the anti-apartheid movement, the governments and organisations that joined with us, not to fight against South Africa as a country or any of its peoples, but to oppose an inhuman system and sue for a speedy end to the apartheid crime against humanity.

These countless human beings, both inside and outside our country, had the nobility of spirit to stand in the path of tyranny and injustice, without seeking selfish gain. They recognised that an injury to one is an injury to all and therefore acted together in defence of justice and a common human decency.

Because of their courage and persistence for many years, we can, today, even set the dates when all humanity will join together to celebrate one of the outstanding human victories of our century.

When that moment comes, we shall, together, rejoice in a common victory over racism, apartheid and white minority rule.

That triumph will finally bring to a close a history of five hundred years of African colonisation that began with the establishment of the Portuguese empire.

Thus, it will mark a great step forward in history and also serve as a common pledge of the peoples of the world to fight racism wherever it occurs and whatever guise it assumes.

At the southern tip of the continent of Africa, a rich reward is in the making, an invaluable gift is in the preparation, for those who suffered in the name of all humanity when they sacrificed everything - for liberty, peace, human dignity and human fulfilment.

This reward will not be measured in money. Nor can it be reckoned in the collective price of the rare metals and precious stones that rest in the bowels of the African soil we tread in the footsteps of our ancestors. It will and must be measured by the happiness and welfare of the children, at once the most vulnerable citizens in any society and the greatest of our treasures.

The children must, at last, play in the open veld, no longer tortured by the pangs of hunger or ravaged by disease or threatened with the scourge of ignorance, molestation and abuse, and no longer required to engage in deeds whose gravity exceeds the demands of their tender years.

In front of this distinguished audience, we commit the new South Africa to the relentless pursuit of the purposes defined in the World Declaration on the Survival, Protection and Development of Children.

The reward of which we have spoken will and must also be measured by the happiness and welfare of the mothers and fathers of these children, who must walk the earth without fear of being robbed, killed for political or material profit, or spat upon because they are beggars.

They too must be relieved of the heavy burden of despair which they carry in their hearts, born of hunger, homelessness and unemployment.

The value of that gift to all who have suffered will and must be measured by the happiness and welfare of all the people of our country, who will have torn down the inhuman walls that divide them.

These great masses will have turned their backs on the grave insult to human dignity which described some as masters and others as servants, and transformed each into a predator whose survival depended on the destruction of the other.

The value of our shared reward will and must be measured by the joyful peace which will triumph, because the common humanity that bonds both black and white into one human race, will have said to each one of us that we shall all live like the children of paradise.

Thus shall we live, because we will have created a society which recognises that all people are born equal, with each entitled in equal measure to life, liberty, prosperity, human rights and good governance.

Such a society should never allow again that there should be prisoners of conscience nor that any person's human rights should be violated.

Neither should it ever happen that once more the avenues to peaceful change are blocked by usurpers who seek to take power away from the people, in pursuit of their own, ignoble purposes.

In relation to these matters, we appeal to those who govern Burma that they release our fellow Nobel Peace Prize laureate, Aung San Suu Kyi, and engage her and those she represents in serious dialogue, for the benefit of all the people of Burma.

We pray that those who have the power to do so will, without further delay, permit that she uses her talents and energies for the greater good of the people of her country and humanity as a whole.

Far from the rough and tumble of the politics of our own country, I would like to take this opportunity to join the Norwegian Nobel Committee and pay tribute to my joint laureate, Mr. F.W. de Klerk.

He had the courage to admit that a terrible wrong had been done to our country and people through the imposition of the system of apartheid.

He had the foresight to understand and accept that all the people of South Africa must, through negotiations and as equal participants in the process, together determine what they want to make of their future.

But there are still some within our country who wrongly believe they can make a contribution to the cause of justice and peace by clinging to the shibboleths that have been proved to spell nothing but disaster.

It remains our hope that these, too, will be blessed with sufficient reason to realise that history will not be denied and that the new society cannot be created by reproducing the repugnant past, however refined or enticingly repackaged.

We live with the hope that as she battles to remake herself, South Africa will be like a microcosm of the new world that is striving to be born.

This must be a world of democracy and respect for human rights, a world freed from the horrors of poverty, hunger, deprivation and ignorance, relieved of the threat and the scourge of civil wars and external aggression and unburdened of the great tragedy of millions forced to become refugees.

The processes in which South Africa and Southern Africa as a whole are engaged, beckon and urge us all that we take this tide at the flood and make of this region a living example of what all people of conscience would like the world to be.

We do not believe that this Nobel Peace Prize is intended as a commendation for matters that have happened and passed.

We hear the voices which say that it is an appeal from all those, throughout the universe, who sought an end to the system of apartheid.

We understand their call, that we devote what remains of our lives to the use of our country's unique and painful experience to demonstrate, in practice, that the normal condition for human existence is democracy, justice, peace, non-racism, non-sexism, prosperity for everybody, a healthy environment and equality and solidarity among the peoples.

Moved by that appeal and inspired by the eminence you have thrust upon us, we undertake that we too will do what we can to contribute to the renewal of our world so that none should, in future, be described as the wretched of the earth.

Let it never be said by future generations that indifference, cynicism or selfishness made us fail to live up to the ideals of humanism which the Nobel Peace Prize encapsulates.

Let the strivings of us all, prove Martin Luther King Jr to have been correct, when he said that humanity can no longer be tragically bound to the starless midnight of racism and war.

Let the efforts of us all, prove that he was not a mere dreamer when he spoke of the beauty of genuine brotherhood and peace being more precious than diamonds or silver or gold.

Let a new age dawn!

Thank you.

JIMMY CARTER
2002

INTRODUCTION

Jimmy Carter (James Earl Carter, Jr.), thirty-ninth president of the United States, was born October 1, 1924, in the small farming town of Plains, Georgia, and grew up in the nearby community of Archery. His father, James Earl Carter, Sr., was a farmer and businessman; his mother, Lillian Gordy, a registered nurse.

He was educated in the Plains public schools, attended Georgia Southwestern College and the Georgia Institute of Technology, and received a B.S. degree from the United States Naval Academy in 1946. In the Navy he became a submariner, serving in both the Atlantic and Pacific fleets and rising to the rank of lieutenant. Chosen by Admiral Hyman Rickover for the nuclear submarine program, he was assigned to Schenectady, N.Y., where he took graduate work at Union College in reactor technology and nuclear physics, and served as senior officer of the pre-commissioning crew of the Seawolf, the second nuclear submarine.

On July 7, 1946, he married Rosalynn Smith of Plains. The Carters have three sons, one daughter, eight grandsons, and three granddaughters. When his father died in 1953, he resigned his naval commission and returned with his family to Georgia. He took over the Carter farms, and he and Rosalynn operated Carter's Warehouse in Plains, a general-purpose seed and farm supply company. He quickly became a leader of the community, serving on county boards supervising education, the hospital authority, and the library. In 1962 he won election to the Georgia Senate. He lost his first gubernatorial campaign in 1966, but won the next election, becoming Georgia's 76th governor on January 12, 1971. He was the Democratic National Committee campaign chairman for the 1974 congressional and gubernatorial elections.

On December 12, 1974, he announced his candidacy for president of the United States. He won his party's nomination on the first ballot at the 1976 Democratic National Convention, and was elected president on November 2, 1976. Jimmy Carter served as president from January 20, 1977 to January 20, 1981.

PRIZE ACCEPTANCE SPEECH

Nobel Lecture, Oslo, December 10, 2002

Former U.S. President Jimmy Carter delivers his Nobel Lecture after receiving the 2002 Nobel Peace Prize in the Oslo City Hall, Oslo, Norway.

Your Majesties, Members of the Norwegian Nobel Committee, Excellencies, Ladies and Gentlemen,

It is with a deep sense of gratitude that I accept this prize. I am grateful to my wife Rosalynn, to my colleagues at The Carter Center, and to many others who continue to seek an end to violence and suffering throughout the world. The scope and character of our Center's activities are perhaps unique, but in many other ways they are typical of the work being done by many hundreds of nongovernmental organizations that strive for human rights and peace.

Most Nobel Laureates have carried out our work in safety, but there are others who have acted with great personal courage. None has provided more vivid reminders of the dangers of peacemaking than two of my friends, Anwar Sadat and Yitzak Rabin, who gave their lives for the cause of peace in the Middle East.

Like these two heroes, my first chosen career was in the military, as a submarine officer. My shipmates and I realized that we had to be ready to fight if combat was forced upon us, and we were prepared to give our lives to defend our nation and its principles. At the same time, we always prayed fervently that our readiness would ensure that there would be no war.

Later, as President and as Commander-in-Chief of our armed forces, I was one of those who bore the sobering responsibility of maintaining global stability during the height of the Cold War, as the world's two superpowers confronted each other. Both sides understood that an unresolved political altercation or a serious misjudgment could lead to a nuclear holocaust. In Washington and in Moscow, we knew that we would have less than a half hour to respond after we learned that intercontinental missiles had been launched against us. There had to be a constant and delicate balancing of our great military strength with aggressive diplomacy, always seeking to build friendships with other nations, large and small, that shared a common cause.

In those days, the nuclear and conventional armaments of the United States and the Soviet Union were almost equal, but democracy ultimately prevailed because of commitments to freedom and human rights, not only by people in my country and those of our allies, but in the former Soviet empire as well. As president, I extended my public support and encouragement to Andrei Sakharov, who, although denied the right to attend the ceremony, was honored here for his personal commitments to these same ideals.

The world has changed greatly since I left the White House. Now there is only one superpower, with unprecedented military and economic strength. The coming budget for American armaments will be greater than those of the next fifteen nations combined, and there are troops from the United States in many countries throughout the world. Our gross national economy exceeds that of the three countries that follow us, and our nation's voice most often prevails as decisions are made concerning trade, humanitarian assistance, and the allocation of global wealth. This dominant status is unlikely to change in our lifetimes.

Great American power and responsibility are not unprecedented, and have been used with restraint and great benefit in the past. We have not assumed that super strength guarantees super wisdom, and we have consistently reached out to the international community to ensure that our own power and influence are tempered by the best common judgment.

Within our country, ultimate decisions are made through democratic means, which tend to moderate radical or ill-advised proposals. Constrained and inspired by historic constitutional principles, our nation has endeavored for more than two hundred years to follow the now almost universal ideals of freedom, human rights, and justice for all.

Our president, Woodrow Wilson, was honored here for promoting the League of Nations, whose two basic concepts were profoundly important: "collective security" and "self-determination." Now they are embedded in international law. Violations of these premises during the last half-century have been tragic failures, as was vividly demonstrated when the Soviet Union attempted to conquer Afghanistan and when Iraq invaded Kuwait.

After the second world war, American Secretary of State Cordell Hull received this prize for his role in founding the United Nations. His successor, General George C. Marshall, was recognized because of his efforts to help rebuild Europe, without excluding the vanquished nations of Italy and Germany. This was a historic example of respecting human rights as the international level.

Ladies and gentlemen:

Twelve years ago, President Mikhail Gorbachev received your recognition for his preeminent role in ending the Cold War that had lasted fifty years.

But instead of entering a millennium of peace, the world is now, in many ways, a more dangerous place. The greater ease of travel and communication has not been matched by equal understanding and mutual respect. There is a plethora of civil wars, unrestrained by rules of the Geneva Convention, within which an overwhelming portion of the casualties are unarmed civilians who have no ability to defend themselves. And recent appalling acts of terrorism have reminded us that no nations, even superpowers, are invulnerable.

It is clear that global challenges must be met with an emphasis on peace, in harmony with others, with strong alliances and international consensus. Imperfect as it may be, there is no doubt that this can best be done through the United Nations, which Ralph Bunche described here in this same forum as exhibiting a "fortunate flexibility" - not merely to preserve peace but also to make change, even radical change, without violence.

He went on to say: "To suggest that war can prevent war is a base play on words and a despicable form of warmongering. The objective of any who sincerely believe in peace clearly must be to exhaust every honorable recourse in the effort to save the peace. The world has had ample evidence that war begets only conditions that beget further war."

We must remember that today there are at least eight nuclear powers on earth, and three of them are threatening to their neighbors in areas of great international tension. For powerful countries to adopt a principle of preventive war may well set an example that can have catastrophic consequences.

If we accept the premise that the United Nations is the best avenue for the maintenance of peace, then the carefully considered decisions of the United Nations Security Council must be enforced. All too often, the alternative has proven to be uncontrollable violence and expanding spheres of hostility.

For more than half a century, following the founding of the State of Israel in 1948, the Middle East conflict has been a source of worldwide tension. At Camp David in 1978 and in Oslo in 1993, Israelis, Egyptians, and Palestinians have endorsed the only reasonable prescription for peace: United Nations Resolution 242. It condemns the acquisition of territory by force, calls for withdrawal of Israel from the occupied territories, and provides for Israelis to live securely and in harmony with their neighbors. There is no other mandate whose implementation could more profoundly improve international relationships.

Perhaps of more immediate concern is the necessity for Iraq to comply fully with the unanimous decision of the Security Council that it eliminate all weapons of mass destruction and permit unimpeded access by inspectors to confirm that this commitment has been honored. The world insists that this be done.

I thought often during my years in the White House of an admonition that we received in our small school in Plains, Georgia, from a beloved teacher, Miss Julia Coleman. She often said: "We must adjust to changing times and still hold to unchanging principles."

When I was a young boy, this same teacher also introduced me to Leo Tolstoy's novel, "War and Peace." She interpreted that powerful narrative as a reminder that the simple human attributes of goodness and truth can overcome great power. She also taught us that an individual is not swept along on a tide of inevitability but can influence even the greatest human events.

These premises have been proven by the lives of many heroes, some of whose names were little known outside their own regions until they became Nobel laureates: Albert John Lutuli, Norman Borlaug, Desmond Tutu, Elie Wiesel, Aung San Suu Kyi, Jody Williams and even Albert Schweitzer and Mother Teresa. All of these and others have proven that even without government power - and often in opposition to it - individuals can enhance human rights and wage peace, actively and effectively.

The Nobel prize also profoundly magnified the inspiring global influence of Martin Luther King, Jr., the greatest leader that my native state has ever produced. On a personal note, it is unlikely that my political career beyond Georgia would have been possible without the changes brought about by the civil rights movement in the American south and throughout our nation.

On the steps of our memorial to Abraham Lincoln, Dr. King said: "I have a dream that on the red hills of Georgia the sons of former slaves and the sons of former slaveowners will be able to sit down together at a table of brotherhood."

The scourge of racism has not been vanquished, either in the red hills of our state or around the world. And yet we see ever more frequent manifestations of his dream of racial healing. In a symbolic but very genuine way, at least involving two Georgians, it is coming true in Oslo today.

I am not here as a public official, but as a citizen of a troubled world who finds hope in a growing consensus that the generally accepted goals of society are peace, freedom, human rights, environmental quality, the alleviation of suffering, and the rule of law.

During the past decades, the international community, usually under the auspices of the United Nations, has struggled to negotiate global standards that can help us achieve these essential goals. They include: the abolition of land mines and chemical weapons; an end to the testing, proliferation, and further deployment of nuclear warheads;

constraints on global warming; prohibition of the death penalty, at least for children; and an international criminal court to deter and to punish war crimes and genocide. Those agreements already adopted must be fully implemented, and others should be pursued aggressively.

We must also strive to correct the injustice of economic sanctions that seek to penalize abusive leaders but all too often inflict punishment on those who are already suffering from the abuse.

The unchanging principles of life predate modern times. I worship Jesus Christ, whom we Christians consider to be the Prince of Peace. As a Jew, he taught us to cross religious boundaries, in service and in love. He repeatedly reached out and embraced Roman conquerors, other Gentiles, and even the more despised Samaritans.

Despite theological differences, all great religions share common commitments that define our ideal secular relationships. I am convinced that Christians, Muslims, Buddhists, Hindus, Jews, and others can embrace each other in a common effort to alleviate human suffering and to espouse peace.

But the present era is a challenging and disturbing time for those whose lives are shaped by religious faith based on kindness toward each other. We have been reminded that cruel and inhuman acts can be derived from distorted theological beliefs, as suicide bombers take the lives of innocent human beings, draped falsely in the cloak of God's will. With horrible brutality, neighbors have massacred neighbors in Europe, Asia, and Africa.

In order for us human beings to commit ourselves personally to the inhumanity of war, we find it necessary first to dehumanize our opponents, which is in itself a violation of the beliefs of all religions. Once we characterize our adversaries as beyond the scope of God's mercy and grace, their lives lose all value. We deny personal responsibility when we plant landmines and, days or years later, a stranger to us - often a child – is crippled or killed. From a great distance, we launch bombs or missiles with almost total impunity, and never want to know the number or identity of the victims.

At the beginning of this new millennium I was asked to discuss, here in Oslo, the greatest challenge that the world faces. Among all the possible choices, I decided that the most serious and universal problem is the growing chasm between the richest and poorest people on earth. Citizens of the ten wealthiest countries are now seventy-five times richer than those who live in the ten poorest ones, and the separation is increasing every year, not only between nations but also within them. The results of this disparity are root causes of most of the world's unresolved problems, including starvation, illiteracy, environmental degradation, violent conflict, and unnecessary illnesses that range from Guinea worm to HIV/AIDS.

Most work of The Carter Center is in remote villages in the poorest nations of Africa, and there I have witnessed the capacity of destitute people to persevere under heartbreaking conditions. I have come to admire their judgment and wisdom, their courage and faith, and their awesome accomplishments when given a chance to use their innate abilities.

But tragically, in the industrialized world there is a terrible absence of understanding or concern about those who are enduring lives of despair and hopelessness. We have not yet made the commitment to share with others an appreciable part of our excessive wealth. This is a potentially rewarding burden that we should all be willing to assume.

Ladies and gentlemen:

War may sometimes be a necessary evil. But no matter how necessary, it is always an evil, never a good. We will not learn how to live together in peace by killing each other's children.

The bond of our common humanity is stronger than the divisiveness of our fears and prejudices. God gives us the capacity for choice. We can choose to alleviate suffering. We can choose to work together for peace. We can make these changes - and we must.

Thank you.

MUHAMMAD YUNUS
2006

INTRODUCTION

Born: 28 June 1940, Birthplace: Chittagong, India (now Bangladesh). Muhammad Yunus earned the nickname "banker to the poor" by giving tiny cash loans — often the equivalent of a few dollars — to the poorest of the poor in Bangladesh. Yunus earned a Ph.D. in economics at Vanderbilt University in 1969.

Yunus and Grameen were jointly given the Nobel Prize in 2006. By that time the bank had helped more than six million borrowers, the vast majority of them women. In awarding the prize, the Nobel Committee stated: "Lasting peace can not be achieved unless large population groups find ways in which to break out of poverty. Microcredit is one such means."

Yunus announced that he would donate his share of the $1.4 million in Nobel prize money to a variety of charities... Grameen means "village" — hence, the village bank... Yunus attended Vanderbilt on a Fulbright scholarship... Yunus's home town of Chittagong was part of India until the Partition of 1947, when the area became East Pakistan. After a 1971 war of independence with Pakistan, the country became known as Bangladesh.

PRIZE ACCEPTANCE SPEECH

Nobel Lecture, Oslo, December 10, 2006.

Your Majesties, Your Royal Highnesses, Honorable Members of the Norwegian Nobel Committee, Excellencies, Ladies and Gentlemen,

Grameen Bank and I are deeply honoured to receive this most prestigious of awards. We are thrilled and overwhelmed by this honour. Since the Nobel Peace Prize was announced, I have received endless messages from around the world, but what moves me most are the calls I get almost daily, from the borrowers of Grameen Bank in remote Bangladeshi villages, who just want to say how proud they are to have received this recognition.

Nine elected representatives of the 7 million borrowers-cum-owners of Grameen Bank have accompanied me all the way to Oslo to receive the prize. I express thanks on their behalf to the Norwegian Nobel Committee for choosing Grameen Bank for this year's Nobel Peace Prize. By giving their institution the most prestigious prize in the world, you give them unparalleled honour. Thanks to your prize, nine proud women from the villages of Bangladesh are at the ceremony today as Nobel laureates, giving an altogether new meaning to the Nobel Peace Prize.

All borrowers of Grameen Bank are celebrating this day as the greatest day of their lives. They are gathering around the nearest television set in their villages all over Bangladesh , along with other villagers, to watch the proceedings of this ceremony.

This years' prize gives highest honour and dignity to the hundreds of millions of women all around the world who struggle every day to make a living and bring hope for a better life for their children. This is a historic moment for them.

Poverty is a Threat to Peace

Ladies and Gentlemen:

By giving us this prize, the Norwegian Nobel Committee has given important support to the proposition that peace is inextricably linked to poverty. Poverty is a threat to peace.

World's income distribution gives a very telling story. Ninety four percent of the world income goes to 40 percent of the population while sixty percent of people live on only 6 per cent of world income. Half of the world population lives on two dollars a day. Over one billion people live on less than a dollar a day. This is no formula for peace.

The new millennium began with a great global dream. World leaders gathered at the United Nations in 2000 and adopted, among others, a historic goal to reduce poverty by half by 2015. Never in human history had such a bold goal been adopted by the entire world in one voice, one that specified time and size. But then came September 11 and the Iraq war, and suddenly the world became derailed from the pursuit of this dream, with the attention of world leaders shifting from the war on poverty to the war on terrorism. Till now over $ 530 billion has been spent on the war in Iraq by the USA alone.

I believe terrorism cannot be won over by military action. Terrorism must be condemned in the strongest language. We must stand solidly against it, and find all the means to end it. We must address the root causes of terrorism to end it for all time to come. I believe that putting resources into improving the lives of the poor people is a better strategy than spending it on guns.

Poverty is Denial of All Human Rights

Peace should be understood in a human way - in a broad social, political and economic way. Peace is threatened by unjust economic, social and political order, absence of democracy, environmental degradation and absence of human rights.

Poverty is the absence of all human rights. The frustrations, hostility and anger generated by abject poverty cannot sustain peace in any society. For building stable peace we must find ways to provide opportunities for people to live decent lives.

The creation of opportunities for the majority of people - the poor - is at the heart of the work that we have dedicated ourselves to during the past 30 years.

Grameen Bank

I became involved in the poverty issue not as a policymaker or a researcher. I became involved because poverty was all around me, and I could not turn away from it. In 1974, I found it difficult to teach elegant theories of economics in the university classroom, in the backdrop of a terrible famine in Bangladesh. Suddenly, I felt the emptiness of those theories in the face of crushing hunger and poverty. I wanted to do something immediate to help people around me, even if it was just one human being, to get through another day with a little more ease. That brought me face to face with poor people's struggle to find the tiniest amounts of money to support their efforts to eke out a living. I was shocked to discover a woman in the village, borrowing less than a dollar from the money-lender, on the condition that he would have the exclusive right to buy all she produces at the price he decides. This, to me, was a way of recruiting slave labor.

I decided to make a list of the victims of this money-lending "business" in the village next door to our campus.

When my list was done, it had the names of 42 victims who borrowed a total amount of US $27. I offered US $27 from my own pocket to get these victims out of the clutches of those money-lenders. The excitement that was created among the people by this small action got me further involved in it. If I could make so many people so happy with such a tiny amount of money, why not do more of it?

That is what I have been trying to do ever since. The first thing I did was to try to persuade the bank located in the campus to lend money to the poor. But that did not work. The bank said that the poor were not creditworthy. After all my efforts, over several months, failed I offered to become a guarantor for the loans to the poor. I was stunned by the result. The poor paid back their loans, on time, every time! But still I kept confronting difficulties in expanding the program through the existing banks. That was when I decided to create a separate bank for the poor, and in 1983, I finally succeeded in doing that. I named it Grameen Bank or Village bank.

Today, Grameen Bank gives loans to nearly 7.0 million poor people, 97 per cent of whom are women, in 73,000 villages in Bangladesh. Grameen Bank gives collateral-free income generating, housing, student and micro-enterprise loans to the poor families and offers a host of attractive savings, pension funds and insurance products for its members. Since it introduced them in 1984, housing loans have been used to construct 640,000 houses. The legal ownership of these houses belongs to the women themselves. We focused on women because we found giving loans to women always brought more benefits to the family.

In a cumulative way the bank has given out loans totaling about US $6.0 billion. The repayment rate is 99%. Grameen Bank routinely makes profit. Financially, it is self-reliant and has not taken donor money since 1995. Deposits and own resources of Grameen Bank today amount to 143 per cent of all outstanding loans. According to Grameen Bank's internal survey, 58 per cent of our borrowers have crossed the poverty line.

Grameen Bank was born as a tiny homegrown project run with the help of several of my students, all local girls and boys. Three of these students are still with me in Grameen Bank, after all these years, as its topmost executives. They are here today to receive this honour you give us.

This idea, which began in Jobra, a small village in Bangladesh, has spread around the world and there are now Grameen type programs in almost every country.

Second Generation

It is 30 years now since we began. We keep looking at the children of our borrowers to see what has been the impact of our work on their lives. The women who are our borrowers always gave topmost priority to the children. One of the Sixteen Decisions developed and followed by them was to send children to school. Grameen Bank encouraged them, and before long all the children were going to school. Many of these children made it to the top of their class. We wanted to celebrate that, so we introduced scholarships for talented students. Grameen Bank now gives 30,000 scholarships every year.

Many of the children went on to higher education to become doctors, engineers, college teachers and other professionals. We introduced student loans to make it easy for Grameen students to complete higher education. Now some of them have PhD's. There are 13,000 students on student loans. Over 7,000 students are now added to this number annually.

We are creating a completely new generation that will be well equipped to take their families way out of the reach of poverty. We want to make a break in the historical continuation of poverty.

Beggars Can Turn to Business

In Bangladesh 80 percent of the poor families have already been reached with microcredit. We are hoping that by 2010, 100 per cent of the poor families will be reached.

Three years ago we started an exclusive programme focusing on the beggars. None of Grameen Bank's rules apply to them. Loans are interest-free; they can pay whatever amount they wish, whenever they wish. We gave them the idea to carry small merchandise such as snacks, toys or household items, when they went from house to house for begging. The idea worked. There are now 85,000 beggars in the program. About 5,000 of them have already stopped begging completely. Typical loan to a beggar is $12.

We encourage and support every conceivable intervention to help the poor fight out of poverty. We always advocate microcredit in addition to all other interventions, arguing that microcredit makes those interventions work better.

Information Technology for the Poor

Information and communication technology (ICT) is quickly changing the world, creating distanceless, borderless world of instantaneous communications. Increasingly, it is becoming less and less costly. I saw an opportunity for the poor people to change their lives if this technology could be brought to them to meet their needs.

As a first step to bring ICT to the poor we created a mobile phone company, Grameen Phone. We gave loans from Grameen Bank to the poor women to buy mobile phones to sell phone services in the villages. We saw the synergy between microcredit and ICT.

The phone business was a success and became a coveted enterprise for Grameen borrowers. Telephone-ladies quickly learned and innovated the ropes of the telephone business, and it has become the quickest way to get out of poverty and to earn social respectability. Today there are nearly 300,000 telephone ladies providing telephone service in all the villages of Bangladesh . Grameen Phone has more than 10 million subscribers, and is the largest mobile phone company in the country. Although the number of telephone-ladies is only a small fraction of the total number of subscribers, they generate 19 per cent of the revenue of the company. Out of the nine board members who are attending this grand ceremony today 4 are telephone-ladies.

Grameen Phone is a joint-venture company owned by Telenor of Norway and Grameen Telecom of Bangladesh. Telenor owns 62 per cent share of the company, Grameen Telecom owns 38 per cent. Our vision was to ultimately convert this company into a social business by giving majority ownership to the poor women of Grameen Bank. We are working towards that goal. Someday Grameen Phone will become another example of a big enterprise owned by the poor.

Free Market Economy

Capitalism centers on the free market. It is claimed that the freer the market, the better is the result of capitalism in solving the questions of what, how, and for whom. It is also claimed that the individual search for personal gains brings collective optimal result.

I am in favor of strengthening the freedom of the market. At the same time, I am very unhappy about the conceptual restrictions imposed on the players in the market. This originates from the assumption that entrepreneurs are one-dimensional human beings, who are dedicated to one mission in their business lives - to maximize profit. This interpretation of capitalism insulates the entrepreneurs from all political, emotional, social, spiritual, environmental dimensions of their lives. This was done perhaps as a reasonable simplification, but it stripped away the very essentials of human life.

Human beings are a wonderful creation embodied with limitless human qualities and capabilities. Our theoretical constructs should make room for the blossoming of those qualities, not assume them away.

Many of the world's problems exist because of this restriction on the players of free-market. The world has not resolved the problem of crushing poverty that half of its population suffers. Healthcare remains out of the reach of the majority of the world population. The country with the richest and freest market fails to provide healthcare for one-fifth of its population.

We have remained so impressed by the success of the free-market that we never dared to express any doubt about our basic assumption. To make it worse, we worked extra hard to transform ourselves, as closely as possible, into the one-dimensional human beings as conceptualized in the theory, to allow smooth functioning of free market mechanism.

By defining "entrepreneur" in a broader way we can change the character of capitalism radically, and solve many of the unresolved social and economic problems within the scope of the free market. Let us suppose an entrepreneur, instead of having a single source of motivation (such as, maximizing profit), now has two sources of motivation, which are mutually exclusive, but equally compelling - a) maximization of profit and b) doing good to people and the world.

Each type of motivation will lead to a separate kind of business. Let us call the first type of business a profit-maximizing business, and the second type of business as social business.

Social business will be a new kind of business introduced in the market place with the objective of making a difference in the world. Investors in the social business could get back their investment, but will not take any dividend from the company. Profit would be ploughed back into the company to expand its outreach and improve the quality of its product or service. A social business will be a non-loss, non-dividend company.

Once social business is recognized in law, many existing companies will come forward to create social businesses in addition to their foundation activities. Many activists from the non-profit sector will also find this an attractive option. Unlike the non-profit sector where one needs to collect donations to keep activities going, a social business will be self-sustaining and create surplus for expansion since it is a non-loss enterprise. Social business will go into a new type of capital market of its own, to raise capital.

Young people all around the world, particularly in rich countries, will find the concept of social business very appealing since it will give them a challenge to make a difference by using their creative talent. Many young people today feel frustrated because they cannot see any worthy challenge, which excites them, within the present capitalist world. Socialism gave them a dream to fight for. Young people dream about creating a perfect world of their own.

Almost all social and economic problems of the world will

be addressed through social businesses. The challenge is to innovate business models and apply them to produce desired social results cost-effectively and efficiently. Healthcare for the poor, financial services for the poor, information technology for the poor, education and training for the poor, marketing for the poor, renewable energy - these are all exciting areas for social businesses.

Social business is important because it addresses very vital concerns of mankind. It can change the lives of the bottom 60 per cent of world population and help them to get out of poverty.

Grameen's Social Business

Even profit maximizing companies can be designed as social businesses by giving full or majority ownership to the poor. This constitutes a second type of social business. Grameen Bank falls under this category of social business.

The poor could get the shares of these companies as gifts by donors, or they could buy the shares with their own money. The borrowers with their own money buy Grameen Bank shares, which cannot be transferred to non-borrowers. A committed professional team does the day-to-day running of the bank.

Bilateral and multi-lateral donors could easily create this type of social business. When a donor gives a loan or a grant to build a bridge in the recipient country, it could create a "bridge company" owned by the local poor. A committed management company could be given the responsibility of running the company. Profit of the company will go to the local poor as dividend, and towards building more bridges. Many infrastructure projects, like roads, highways, airports, seaports, utility companies could all be built in this manner.

Grameen has created two social businesses of the first type. One is a yogurt factory, to produce fortified yogurt to bring nutrition to malnourished children, in a joint venture with Danone. It will continue to expand until all malnourished children of Bangladesh are reached with this yogurt. Another is a chain of eye-care hospitals. Each hospital will undertake 10,000 cataract surgeries per year at differentiated prices to the rich and the poor.

Social Stock Market

To connect investors with social businesses, we need to create social stock market where only the shares of social businesses will be traded. An investor will come to this stock-exchange with a clear intention of finding a social business, which has a mission of his liking. Anyone who wants to make money will go to the existing stock-market.

To enable a social stock-exchange to perform properly, we will need to create rating agencies, standardization of terminology, definitions, impact measurement tools, reporting formats, and new financial publications, such as, *The Social Wall Street Journal.* Business schools will offer courses and business management degrees on social businesses to train young managers how to manage social business enterprises in the most efficient manner, and, most of all, to inspire them to become social business entrepreneurs themselves.

Role of Social Businesses in Globalization

I support globalization and believe it can bring more benefits to the poor than its alternative. But it must be the right kind of globalization. To me, globalization is like a hundred-lane highway criss-crossing the world. If it is a free-for-all highway, its lanes will be taken over by the giant trucks from powerful economies. Bangladeshi rickshaw will be thrown off the highway. In order to have a win-win globalization we must have traffic rules, traffic police, and traffic authority for this global highway. Rule of "strongest takes it all" must be replaced by rules that ensure that the poorest have a place and piece of the action, without being elbowed out by the strong. Globalization must not become financial imperialism.

Powerful multi-national social businesses can be created to retain the benefit of globalization for the poor people and poor countries. Social businesses will either bring ownership to the poor people, or keep the profit within the poor countries, since taking dividends will not be their objective. Direct foreign investment by foreign social businesses will be exciting news for recipient countries. Building strong economies in the poor countries by protecting their national interest from plundering companies will be a major area of interest for the social businesses.

We Create What We Want

We get what we want, or what we don't refuse. We accept the fact that we will always have poor people around us, and that poverty is part of human destiny. This is precisely why we continue to have poor people around us. If we firmly believe that poverty is unacceptable to us, and that it should not belong to a civilized society, we would have built appropriate institutions and policies to create a poverty-free world.

We wanted to go to the moon, so we went there. We achieve what we want to achieve. If we are not achieving something, it is because we have not put our minds to it. We create what we want.

What we want and how we get to it depends on our mindsets. It is extremely difficult to change mindsets once they are formed. We create the world in accordance with our mindset. We need to invent ways to change our perspective continually and reconfigure our mindset quickly as new knowledge emerges. We can reconfigure our world if we can reconfigure our mindset.

We Can Put Poverty in the Museums

I believe that we can create a poverty-free world because poverty is not created by poor people. It has been created and sustained by the economic and social system that we have designed for ourselves; the institutions and concepts that make up that system; the policies that we pursue.

Poverty is created because we built our theoretical framework on assumptions which under-estimates human capacity, by designing concepts, which are too narrow (such as concept of business, credit- worthiness, entrepreneurship, employment) or developing institutions, which remain half-done (such as financial institutions, where poor are left out). Poverty is caused by the failure at the conceptual level, rather than any lack of capability on the part of people.

I firmly believe that we can create a poverty-free world if we collectively believe in it. In a poverty-free world, the only place you would be able to see poverty is in the poverty museums. When school children take a tour of the poverty museums, they would be horrified to see the misery and indignity that some human beings had to go through. They would blame their forefathers for tolerating this inhuman condition, which existed for so long, for so many people.

A human being is born into this world fully equipped not only to take care of him or herself, but also to contribute to enlarging the well being of the world as a whole. Some get the chance to explore their potential to some degree, but many others never get any opportunity, during their lifetime, to unwrap the wonderful gift they were born with. They die unexplored and the world remains deprived of their creativity, and their contribution.

Grameen has given me an unshakeable faith in the creativity of human beings. This has led me to believe that human beings are not born to suffer the misery of hunger and poverty.

To me poor people are like bonsai trees. When you plant the best seed of the tallest tree in a flower-pot, you get a replica of the tallest tree, only inches tall. There is nothing wrong with the seed you planted, only the soil-base that is too inadequate. Poor people are bonsai people. There is nothing wrong in their seeds. Simply, society never gave them the base to grow on. All it needs to get the poor people out of poverty for us to create an enabling environment for them. Once the poor can unleash their energy and creativity, poverty will disappear very quickly.

Let us join hands to give every human being a fair chance to unleash their energy and creativity.

Ladies and Gentlemen,

Let me conclude by expressing my deep gratitude to the Norwegian Nobel Committee for recognizing that poor people, and especially poor women, have both the potential and the right to live a decent life, and that microcredit helps to unleash that potential.

I believe this honor that you give us will inspire many more bold initiatives around the world to make a historical breakthrough in ending global poverty.

Thank you very much.

ALBERT ARNOLD (AL) GORE JR.
2007

INTRODUCTION

Former Vice President Al Gore is cofounder and Chairman of Generation Investment Management, a firm that is focused on a new approach to Sustainable Investing.

Gore is also cofounder and Chairman of Current TV, an independently owned cable and satellite television network for young people based on viewer-created content and citizen journalism. A member of the Board of Directors of Apple Computer, Inc. and a Senior Advisor to Google, Inc. Gore is also Visiting Professor at Middle Tennessee State University in Murfreesboro, Tennessee.

Mr. Gore is the author of *An Inconvenient Truth*, a best-selling book on the threat of and solutions to global warming, and the subject of the movie of the same title, which has already become one of the top documentary films in history. In 2007, An Inconvenient Truth was awarded two Academy Awards for Best Documentary Feature and Best Original Song.

Since his earliest days in the U. S. Congress 30 years ago, Al Gore has been the leading advocate for confronting the threat of global warming. His pioneering efforts were outlined in his best-selling book *Earth in the Balance: Ecology and the Human Spirit* (1992). He led the Clinton-Gore Administration's efforts to protect the environment in a way that also strengthens the economy.

Al Gore was born on March 31, 1948, the son of former U.S. Senator Albert Gore, Sr. and Pauline Gore. Raised in Carthage,

Tennessee, and Washington, D.C., he received a degree in government with honors from Harvard University in 1969. After graduation, he volunteered for enlistment in the U.S. Army and served in the Vietnam War. Upon returning from Vietnam, Al Gore became an investigative reporter with the Tennessean in Nashville, where he also attended Vanderbilt University's Divinity School and then Law School.

Al Gore and his wife, Tipper, reside in Nashville, Tennessee. They have four children- Karenna, Kristin, Sarah, and Albert III; and two grandchildren: Wyatt Gore Schiff and Anna Hunger Schiff.

Nobel Peace Prize for 2007 to be shared, in two equal parts, between the Intergovernmental Panel on Climate Change (IPCC) and Albert Arnold (Al) Gore Jr. for their efforts to build up and disseminate greater knowledge about man-made climate change, and to lay the foundations for the measures that are needed to counteract such change.

PRIZE ACCEPTANCE SPEECH

Nobel Lecture, Oslo, 10 December 2007.

Your Majesties, Your Royal Highnesses, Honorable members of the Norwegian Nobel Committee, Excellencies, Ladies and gentlemen.

I have a purpose here today. It is a purpose I have tried to serve for many years. I have prayed that God would show me a way to accomplish it.

Sometimes, without warning, the future knocks on our door with a precious and painful vision of what might be. One hundred and nineteen years ago, a wealthy inventor read his own obituary, mistakenly published years before his death. Wrongly believing the inventor had just died, a newspaper printed a harsh judgment of his life's work, unfairly labeling him "The Merchant of Death" because of his invention – dynamite. Shaken by this condemnation, t he inventor made a fateful choice to serve the cause of peace.

Seven years later, Alfred Nobel created this prize and the others that bear his name.

Seven years ago tomorrow, I read my own political obituary in a judgment that seemed to me harsh and mistaken – if not premature. But that unwelcome verdict also brought a precious if painful gift: an opportunity to search for fresh new ways to serve my purpose.

Unexpectedly, that quest has brought me here. Even though I fear my words cannot match this moment, I pray what I am feeling in my heart will be communicated clearly enough that those who hear me will say, "We must act."

The distinguished scientists with whom it is the greatest honor of my life to share this award have laid before us a choice between two different futures – a choice that to my ears echoes the words of an ancient prophet: "Life or death, blessings or curses. Therefore, choose life, that both thou and thy seed may live."

We, the human species, are confronting a planetary emergency – a threat to the survival of our civilization that is gathering ominous and destructive potential even as we gather here. But there is hopeful news as well: we have the ability to solve this crisis and avoid the worst – though not all – of its consequences, if we act boldly, decisively and quickly.

However, despite a growing number of honorable exceptions, too many of the world's leaders are still best described in the words Winston Churchill applied to those who ignored Adolf Hitler's threat: "They go on in strange paradox, decided only to be undecided, resolved to be irresolute, adamant for drift, solid for fluidity, all powerful to be impotent."

So today, we dumped another 70 million tons of global-warming pollution into the thin shell of atmosphere surrounding our planet, as if it were an open sewer. And tomorrow, we will dump a slightly larger amount, with the cumulative concentrations now trapping more and more heat from the sun.

As a result, the earth has a fever. And the fever is rising. The experts have told us it is not a passing affliction that will heal by itself. We asked for a second opinion. And a third. And a fourth. And the consistent conclusion, restated with increasing alarm, is that something basic is wrong.

We are what is wrong, and we must make it right.

Last September 21, as the Northern Hemisphere tilted away from the sun, scientists reported with unprecedented distress that the North Polar ice cap is "falling off a cliff."

One study estimated that it could be completely gone during summer in less than 22 years. Another new study, to be presented by U.S. Navy researchers later this week, warns it could happen in as little as 7 years.

Seven years from now.

In the last few months, it has been harder and harder to misinterpret the signs that our world is spinning out of kilter. Major cities in North and South America, Asia and Australia are nearly out of water due to massive droughts and melting glaciers. Desperate farmers are losing their livelihoods. Peoples in the frozen Arctic and on low-lying Pacific islands are planning evacuations of places they have long called home. Unprecedented wildfires have forced a half million people from their homes in one country and caused a national emergency that almost brought down the government in another. Climate refugees have migrated into areas already inhabited by people with different cultures, religions, and traditions, increasing the potential for conflict. Stronger storms in the Pacific and Atlantic have threatened whole cities. Millions have been displaced by massive flooding in South Asia, Mexico, and 18 countries in Africa. As temperature extremes have increased, tens of thousands have lost their lives. We are recklessly burning and clearing our forests and driving more and more species into extinction. The very web of life on which we depend is being ripped and frayed.

We never intended to cause all this destruction, just as Alfred Nobel never intended that dynamite be used for waging war. He had hoped his invention would promote human progress. We shared that same worthy goal when we began burning massive quantities of coal, then oil and methane.

Even in Nobel's time, there were a few warnings of the likely consequences. One of the very first winners of the Prize in chemistry worried that, "We are evaporating our coal mines into the air." After performing 10,000 equations by hand, Svante Arrhenius calculated that the earth's average temperature would increase by many degrees if we doubled the amount of CO2 in the atmosphere.

Seventy years later, my teacher, Roger Revelle, and his colleague, Dave Keeling, began to precisely document the increasing CO2 levels day by day.

But unlike most other forms of pollution, CO_2 is invisible, tasteless, and odorless – which has helped keep the truth about what it is doing to our climate out of sight and out of mind. Moreover, the catastrophe now threatening us is unprecedented – and we often confuse the unprecedented with the improbable.

We also find it hard to imagine making the massive changes that are now necessary to solve the crisis. And when large truths are genuinely inconvenient, whole societies can, at least for a time, ignore them. Yet as George Orwell reminds us: "Sooner or later a false belief bumps up against solid reality, usually on a battlefield."

In the years since this prize was first awarded, the entire relationship between humankind and the earth has been radically transformed. And still, we have remained largely oblivious to the impact of our cumulative actions.

Indeed, without realizing it, we have begun to wage war on the earth itself. Now, we and the earth's climate are locked in a relationship familiar to war planners: "Mutually assured destruction."

More than two decades ago,scientistscalculated thatnuclear war could throw so much debris and smoke into the air that it would block life-giving sunlight from our atmosphere, causing a "nuclear winter." Their eloquent warnings here in Oslo helped galvanize the world's resolve to halt the nuclear arms race.

Now science is warning us that if we do not quickly reduce the global warming pollution that is trapping so much of the heat our planet normally radiates back out of the atmosphere, we are in danger of creating a permanent "carbon summer."

As the American poet Robert Frost wrote, " Some say the world will end in fire; some say in ice." Either, he notes, "would suffice."

But neither need be our fate.It is time to make peace with the planet.

We must quickly mobilize our civilization with the urgency and resolve that has previously been seen only when nations mobilized for war. These prior struggles for survival were won when leaders found words at the 11th hour that released a mighty surge of courage, hope and readiness to sacrifice for a protracted and mortal challenge.

These were not comforting and misleading assurances that the threat was not real or imminent; that it would affect others but not ourselves; that ordinary life might be lived even in the presence of extraordinary threat; thatProvidence could be trusted to do for us what we would not do for ourselves.

No, these were calls to come to the defense of the common future. They were calls upon the courage, generosity and strength of entire peoples, citizens of every class and condition who were ready to stand against the threat once asked to do so. Our enemies in those times calculated that free people would not rise to the challenge; they were, of course, catastrophically wrong.

Now comes the threat of climate crisis – a threat that is real, rising, imminent, and universal. Once again, it is the 11th hour. The penaltiesfor ignoring this challenge are immense and growing, and at some near point would be unsustainable and unrecoverable. For now we still have the power to choose our fate, and the remaining question is only this: Have we the will to act vigorously and in time, or will we remain imprisoned by a dangerous illusion?

Mahatma Gandhi awakened the largest democracy on earth and forged a shared resolve with what he called "Satyagraha" – or "truth force."

In every land, the truth – once known – has the power to set us free.

Truth also has the power to unite us and bridge the distance between "me" and "we," creating the basis for common effort and shared responsibility.

There is an African proverb that says, "If you want to go quickly, go alone. If you want to go far, go together." We need to go far, quickly.

We must abandon the conceit that individual, isolated, private actions are the answer. They can and do help. But they will not take us far enough without collective action. At the same time, we must ensure that in mobilizing globally, we do not invite the establishment of ideological conformity and a new lock-step "ism."

That means adopting principles, values, laws, and treaties that release creativity and initiative at every level of society in multifold responses originating concurrently and spontaneously.

This new consciousness requires expanding the possibilities inherent in all humanity. The innovators who will devise a new way to harness the sun's energy for pennies or invent an engine that's carbon negative may live in Lagos or Mumbai or Montevideo. We must ensure that entrepreneurs and inventors everywhere on the globe have the chance to change the world.

When we unite for a moral purpose that is manifestly good and true, the spiritual energy unleashed can transform us. The generation that defeated fascism throughout the world in the 1940s found, in rising to meet their awesome challenge, that they had gained the moral authority and long-term vision to launch the Marshall Plan, the United Nations, and a new level of global cooperation and foresight that unified Europe and facilitated the emergence of democracy and prosperity in Germany, Japan, Italy and much of the world. One of their visionary leaders said, "It is time we steered by the stars and not by the lights of every passing ship."

In the last year of that war, you gave the Peace Prize to a man from my hometown of 2000 people, Carthage, Tennessee. Cordell Hull was described by Franklin Roosevelt as the "Father of the United Nations." He was an inspiration and hero to my own father, who followed Hull in the Congress and the U.S. Senate and in his commitment to world peace and global cooperation.

My parents spoke often of Hull, always in tones of reverence and admiration. Eight weeks ago, when you announced this prize, the deepest emotion I felt was when I saw the headline in my hometown paper that simply noted I had won the same prize that Cordell Hull had won. I n that moment, I knew what my father and mother would have felt were they alive.

Just as Hull's generation found moral authority in rising to solve the world crisis caused by fascism, so too can we find our greatest opportunity in rising to solve the climate crisis. In the Kanji characters used in both Chinese and Japanese, "crisis" is written with two symbols, the first meaning "danger," the second "opportunity." By facing and removing the danger of the climate crisis, we have the opportunity to gain the moral authority and vision to vastly increase our own capacity to solve other crises that have been too long ignored.

We must understand the connections between the climate crisis and the afflictions of poverty, hunger, HIV-Aids and other pandemics. As these problems are linked, so too must be their solutions. We must begin by making the common rescue of the global environment the central organizing principle of the world community.

Fifteen years ago, I made that case at the "Earth Summit" in Rio de Janeiro. Ten years ago, I presented it in Kyoto. This week, I will urge the delegates in Bali to adopt a bold mandate for a treaty that establishes a universal global cap on emissions and uses the market in emissions trading to efficiently allocate resources to the most effective opportunities for speedy reductions.

This treaty should be ratified and brought into effect everywhere in the world by the beginning of 2010 – two years sooner than presently contemplated. The pace of our response must be accelerated to match the accelerating pace of the crisis itself.

Heads of state should meet early next year to review what was accomplished in Bali and take personal responsibility for addressing this crisis. It is not unreasonable to ask, given the gravity of our circumstances, that these heads of state meet every three months until the treaty is completed.

We also need a moratorium on the construction of any new generating facility that burns coal without the capacity to safely trap and store carbon dioxide.

And most important of all, we need to put a *price* on carbon – with a CO2 tax that is then rebated back to the people, progressively, according to the laws of each nation, in ways that shift the burden of taxation from employment to pollution. This is by far the most effective and simplest way to accelerate solutions to this crisis.

The world needs an alliance – especially of those nations that weigh heaviest in the scales where earth is in the balance. I salute Europe and Japan for the steps they've taken in recent years to meet the challenge, and the new government in Australia, which has made solving the climate crisis its first priority.

But the outcome will be decisively influenced by two nations that are now failing to do enough: the United States and China. While India is also growing fast in importance, it should be absolutely clear that it is the two largest CO2 emitters – most of all, my own country – that will need to make the boldest moves, or stand accountable before history for their failure to act.

Both countries should stop using the other's behavior as an excuse for stalemate and instead develop an agenda for mutual survival in a shared global environment.

These are the last few years of decision, but they can be the first years of a bright and hopeful future if we do what we must. No one should believe a solution will be found without effort, without cost, without change. Let us acknowledge that if we wish toredeem squandered time and speak again with moral authority, then these are the hard truths:

The way ahead is difficult. The outer boundary of what we currently believe is feasible is still far short of what we actually must do. Moreover, between here and there, across the unknown, falls the shadow.

That is just another way of saying that we have to expand the boundaries of what is possible. In the words of the Spanish poet, Antonio Machado, "Pathwalker, there is no path. You must make the path as you walk."

We are standing at the most fateful fork in that path. So I want to end as I began, with a vision of two futures – each a palpable possibility – and with a prayer that we will see with vivid clarity the necessity of choosing between those two futures, and the urgency of making the right choice now.

The great Norwegian playwright, Henrik Ibsen, wrote, "One of these days, the younger generation will come knocking at my door."

The future is knocking at our door right now. Make no mistake, the next generation *will* ask us one of two questions. Either they will ask: "What were you thinking; why didn't you act? "

Or they will ask instead: "How did you find the moral courage to rise and successfully resolve a crisis that so many said was impossible to solve?"

We have everything we need to get started, save perhaps political will, but political will is a renewable resource.

So let us renew it, and say together: "We have a purpose. We are many. For this purpose we will rise, and we will act."

LIU XIAOBO
2010

INTRODUCTION

Liu Xiaobo (born 28 December 1955) is a Chinese literary critic, writer, professor, and human rights activist who called for political reforms and the end of communist single-party rule. He is currently incarcerated as a political prisoner in Jinzhou, Liaoning.

Liu has served from 2003 to 2007 as President of the Independent Chinese PEN Center. He was also the President of MinZhuZhongGuo (Democratic China) magazine since the mid-1990s. On 8 December 2008, Liu was detained because of his participation with the Charter 08 manifesto. He was formally arrested on 23 June 2009 on suspicion of "inciting subversion of state power." He was tried on the same charges on 23 December 2009, and sentenced to eleven years' imprisonment and two years' deprivation of political rights on 25 December 2009.

During his fourth prison term, he was awarded the 2010 Nobel Peace Prize for "his long and non-violent struggle for fundamental human rights in China." He is the first Chinese citizen to be awarded a Nobel Prize of any kind while residing in China. Liu is the third person to be awarded the Nobel Peace Prize while in prison or detention, after Germany's Carl von Ossietzky (1935) and Burma's Aung San Suu Kyi (1991). Liu is also the second person (the first being Ossietzky) to be denied the right to have a representative collect the Nobel prize for him.

PRIZE ACCEPTANCE SPEECH

Presentation Speech by Thorbjørn Jagland, Chairman of the Norwegian Nobel Committee, Oslo, 10 December 2010.

Your Majesties, Excellencies, Ladies and Gentlemen,

"The Norwegian Nobel Committee has decided to award the Nobel Peace Prize for 2010 to Liu Xiaobo for his long and non-violent struggle for fundamental human rights in China. The Norwegian Nobel Committee has long believed that there is a close connection between human rights and peace. Such rights are a prerequisite for the "fraternity between nations" of which Alfred Nobel wrote in his will."

This was the first paragraph of the Norwegian Nobel Committee's announcement on the 8th of October of the award of this year's Peace Prize.

We regret that the Laureate is not present here today. He is in isolation in a prison in north-east China. Nor can the Laureate's wife Liu Xia or his closest relatives be here with us. No medal or diploma will therefore be presented here today.

This fact alone shows that the award was necessary and appropriate. We congratulate Liu Xiaobo on this year's Peace Prize.

There have been a number of previous occasions when the Laureate has been prevented from attending. This has in fact been the case with several awards which have proved in the light of history to have been most significant and honourable. Even when the Laureate has come, he or she has several times been severely condemned by the authorities of his or her own country.

There was a great deal of trouble in 1935, when the Committee gave the award to Carl von Ossietzky. Hitler was furious, and prohibited all Germans from accepting any Nobel Prize. King Haakon did not attend the ceremony. Ossietzky did not come to Oslo, and died a little over a year later.

There was considerable outrage in Moscow when Andrej Sakharov received his Prize in 1975. He, too, was prevented from receiving the award in person. He sent his wife. The same thing happened to Lech Walesa in 1983. The Burmese authorities were furious when Aung San Suu Kyi received the Peace Prize in 1991. Once again, the Laureate could not come to Oslo.

In 2003, Shirin Ebadi received the Nobel Peace Prize. She came. Much could be said of the reaction of the Iranian authorities, but the Iranian Ambassador did in fact attend the ceremony.

The Norwegian Nobel Committee has given four Prizes to South Africa. All the Laureates came to Oslo, but the awards to Albert Lutuli in 1960 and to Desmond Tutu in 1984 provoked great outrage in the apartheid regime in South Africa, before the applause broke out thanks to the awards to Nelson Mandela and F.W. de Klerk in 1993.

The point of these awards has of course never been to offend anyone. The Nobel Committee's intention has been to say something about the relationship between human rights, democracy and peace. And it has been important to remind the world that the rights so widely enjoyed today were fought for and won by persons who took great risks.

They did so for others. That is why Liu Xiaobo deserves our support.

Although none of the Committee's members have ever met Liu, we feel that we know him. We have studied him closely over a long period of time.

Liu was born on the 28th of December 1955 in Changchun in China's Jilin province. He took a Bachelor's degree in literature at Jilin University, and a Master's degree and a PhD at Beijing Normal University, where he also taught. Stays abroad included visits to Oslo, Hawaii, and Columbia University, New York.

In 1989 he returned home to take part in the dawning democracy movement. On the 2nd of June he and some friends started a hunger strike on Tiananmen Square to protest against the state of emergency that had been declared. They issued a six-point democratic manifesto, written by Liu, opposing dictatorship and in favour of democracy. Liu was opposed to any physical struggle against the authorities on the part of the students; he tried to find a peaceful solution to the tension between the students and the government. Non-violence was already figuring prominently in his message. On the 4th of June he and his friends tried to prevent a clash between the army and the students. He was only partially successful. Many lives were lost, most of them outside Tiananmen Square.

Liu has told his wife that he would like this year's Peace Prize to be dedicated to "the lost souls from the 4th of June." It is a pleasure for us to fulfil his wish.

Liu has said that "The greatness of non-violent resistance is that even as man is faced with forceful tyranny and the resulting suffering, the victim responds to hate with love, to prejudice with tolerance, to arrogance with humility, to humiliation with dignity, and to violence with reason."

Tiananmen became a turning-point in Liu's life.

In 1996, Liu was sentenced to three years in a labour camp for "rumour-mongering and slander." He was president of the independent Chinese PEN-centre from 2003 to 2007. Liu has written nearly 800 essays, 499 of them since 2005. He was one of the chief architects behind Charter 08, which was made known on the 10th of December 2008, which was, in the words of the document's Preamble, on the occasion of "the one hundredth anniversary of China's first Constitution, the 60th anniversary of the promulgation of the Universal Declaration of Human Rights, the 30th anniversary of the birth of the Democracy Wall, and the 10th anniversary of the Chinese government's signature of the International Covenant on Civil and Political Rights." Charter 08 defends fundamental human rights and has in due course been signed by several thousand persons both in China itself and abroad.

On the 25th of December 2009, Liu was sentenced to 11 years' imprisonment and two years' loss of political rights for, in the words of the sentence, "incitement to the overthrow of the state power and socialist system and the people's democratic dictatorship." Liu has consistently claimed that the sentence violates both China's own constitution and fundamental human rights.

There are many dissidents in China, and their opinions differ on many points. The severe punishment imposed on Liu made him more than a central spokesman for human rights. Practically overnight, he became the very symbol, both in China and internationally, of the struggle for such rights in China.

Your Majesties, ladies and gentlemen,

During the cold war, the connections between peace and human rights were disputed. Since the end of the cold war, however, peace researchers and political scientists have almost without exception underlined how close those connections are. This is, allegedly, one of the most "robust" findings they have arrived at. Democracies may go to war against dictatorships, and have certainly waged colonial wars, but there is, apparently, not a single example of a democracy having gone to war against another democracy.

The deeper "fraternity between nations" which Alfred Nobel mentions in his will, and which is a prerequisite for real peace, can hardly be created without human rights and democracy.

There are scarcely any examples in world history of a great power achieving such rapid growth over such a long period of time as China. Since 1978, year by year, decade after decade, the country's growth rate has stood at 10 percent or more. A few years ago the country's output was greater than Germany's; this year it exceeded Japan's. China has thus achieved the world's second largest gross national product. The USA's national product is still three times greater than China's, but while China is continuing its advance, the USA is in serious difficulties.

Economic success has lifted several hundred million Chinese out of poverty. For the reduction in the number of poor people in the world, China must be given the main credit.

We can to a certain degree say that China with its 1.3 billion people is carrying mankind's fate on its shoulders. If the country proves capable of developing a social market economy with full civil rights, this will have a huge favourable impact on the world. If not, there is a danger of social and economic crises arising in the country, with negative consequences for us all.

Historical experience gives us reason to believe that continuing rapid economic growth presupposes opportunities for free research, thinking and debate. And moreover: without freedom of expression, corruption, the abuse of power, and misrule will develop. Every power system must be counterbalanced by popularly elected control, free media, and the right of individual citizens to criticise.

More or less authoritarian states may have long periods of rapid economic growth, but it is no coincidence that nearly all the richest countries in the world are democratic. Democracy mobilises new human and technological resources.

China's new status entails increased responsibility. China must be prepared for criticism and regard it as positive – as an opportunity for improvement. This must be the case wherever there is great power. We have all formed opinions on the role of the USA through the years. Friends and allies criticised the country both for the Vietnam War and for the lack of civil rights for the coloured people. Many Americans were opposed to the award of the Nobel Peace Prize to Martin Luther King in 1964. Looking back, we can see that the USA grew stronger when the African-American people obtained their rights.

Many will ask whether China's weakness – for all the strength the country is currently showing – is not manifested in the need to imprison a man for eleven years merely for expressing his opinions on how his country should be governed.

This weakness finds clear expression in the sentence on Liu, where it is underlined as especially serious that he spread his opinions on the Internet. But those who fear technological advances have every reason to fear the future. Information technology can not be abolished. It will continue to open societies. As Russia's President Dmitrij Medvedev put it in an address to the Duma: "The new information technology gives us an opportunity to become connected with the world. The world and society are growing more open even if the ruling class does not like it."

No doubt Medvedev had the fate of the Soviet Union in mind. Compulsory uniformity and control of thought prevented the country from participating in the technological revolution which took place in the 1970s and 80s. The system broke down. The country would have stood to gain a great deal more from entering into a dialogue at an early stage with people like Andrej Sakharov.

Your Majesties, ladies and gentlemen,

Today neither the nation-state nor a majority within the nation-state has unlimited authority. Human rights limit what the nation-state and the majority in a nation-state can do. This must apply to all states that are members of the United Nations and who have acceded to the Universal Declaration of Human Rights. China has signed and even ratified several of the UN's and the ILO's major international conventions on human rights. It is interesting that China has accepted the supranational conflict-resolving mechanism of the WTO.

China's own constitution upholds fundamental human rights. Article 35 of the country's constitution thus lays down that "Citizens of the People's Republic of China enjoy freedom of speech, of the press, of assembly, of association, of procession and of demonstration." Article 41 begins by stating that citizens "...have the right to criticise and make suggestions regarding any state organ or functionary."

Liu has exercised his civil rights. He has done nothing wrong. He must therefore be released!

In the past 100 to 150 years, human rights and democracy have gained an ever-stronger position in the world. And with them, peace. This can be clearly seen in Europe, where so many wars were fought, and whose colonial powers started so many wars around the world. Europe today is on the whole a continent of "peace". Decolonization after the Second World War gave a number of countries, first in Asia and then in Africa, the chance to govern themselves with respect for basic human rights. With India in the lead, many of them seized the opportunity. Over the latest decades, we have seen how democracy has consolidated its position in Latin America and in Central and Eastern Europe. Many countries in the Muslim part of the world are treading the same path: Turkey, Indonesia, Malaysia. Several other countries are in the process of opening up their political systems.

The human rights activists in China are defenders of the international order and the main trends in the global community. Viewed in that light, they are thus not dissidents, but representatives of the main lines of development in today's world.

Liu denies that criticism of the Communist Party is the same as offending China and the Chinese people. He argues that "Even if the Communist Party is the ruling party, it cannot be equated with the country, let alone with the nation and its culture." Changes in China can take time, a very long time: political reforms should, as Liu says, " be gradual, peaceful, orderly and controlled." China has had enough of attempts at revolutionary change. They only lead to chaos. But as Liu also writes, "An enormous transformation towards pluralism in society has already taken place, and official authority is no longer able to fully control the whole society." However strong the power of the regime may appear to be, every single individual must do his best to live, in his words, "an honest life with dignity."

The answer from the Chinese authorities is to claim that this year's Peace Prize humiliates China, and to give very derogatory descriptions of Liu.

History shows many examples of political leaders playing on nationalist feelings and attempting to demonize holders of contrary opinions. They soon become foreign agents. This has sometimes happened in the name of democracy and freedom, but almost always with a tragic outcome.

We recognise this in the rhetoric of the struggle against terrorism: "You are either for me or against me." Such undemocratic methods as torture and imprisonment without sentence have been used in the name of freedom. This has led to more polarisation of the world and harmed the fight against terrorism.

Liu Xiaobo is an optimist, despite his many years in prison. In his closing appeal to the court on the 23rd of December 2009, he said: "I, filled with optimism, look forward to the advent of a future free China. For there is no force that can put an end to the human quest for freedom, and China will in the end become a nation ruled by law, where human rights reign supreme."

Isaac Newton once said, "If I have seen further, it is by standing on the shoulders of giants." When we are able to look ahead today, it is because we are standing on the shoulders of the many men and women who over the years – often at great risk – have stood up for what they believed in and thus made our freedom possible.

Therefore: while others at this time are counting their money, focussing exclusively on their short-term national interests, or remaining indifferent, the Norwegian Nobel Committee has once again chosen to support those who fight – for us all. We congratulate Liu Xiaobo on the Nobel Peace Prize for 2010. His views will in the long run strengthen China. We extend to him and to China our very best wishes for the years ahead.

ECONOMICS

JAN TINBERGEN
1969

INTRODUCTION

Jan Tinbergen (The Hague, April 12, 1903 – June 9, 1994 The Hague), Dutch economist, was awarded the first Bank of Sweden Prize in Economic Sciences in Memory of Alfred Nobel in 1969, which he shared with Ragnar Frisch for having developed and applied dynamic models for the analysis of economic processes.

In 1929 he earned his PhD with his thesis entitled "Minimumproblemen in de natuurkunde en de economie" (Minimisation problems in Physics and Economics). From 1929 till 1945 he worked, in addition to his professorship at Erasmus University Rotterdam, for the Dutch statistical office.

He was also consultant to the League of Nations. From 1945 till 1955 he served as the first director of the Netherlands Bureau for Economic Policy Analysis. Jan Tinbergen was a member of the Royal Netherlands Academy of Arts and Science and of the International Academy of Science.

Tinbergen developed the first national comprehensive macroeconomic model, which he first built for the Netherlands and later applied to the United States and the United Kingdom after World War II. His younger brothers Nikolaas and Luuk were important ornithologists, and Nikolaas won the Nobel Prize in Physiology or Medicine. Tinbergen founded the Econometric Institute at the Erasmus Universiteit Rotterdam.

PRIZE ACCEPTANCE SPEECH

Jan Tinbergen's speech at the Nobel Banquet in Stockholm, December 10, 1969

Your Majesty, Your Royal Highnesses, Your Excellencies, Ladies and Gentlemen,

I feel that I should speak in the name of three entities, if I may say so. First of all in the name of all economists, that it looks as if from now on economics has become a grown-up science. We are very grateful to Riksbanken and the Nobel foundation for having agreed that with Riksbanken's gift and applying the rules of the Nobel Foundation it will be possible in the future to have a prize for economics, the Alfred Nobel Memorial Prize for Economics.

Within the group of economists I think I should speak a special word in the name of those who are calling themselves econometricians, those who apply mathematics and statistics together with economics in order to verify economic theories and therefore, as we think, to contribute to making scientific work possible at a higher stage in economics.

But then I would like to add, and here I follow one of my colleagues and predecessors, to say that I myself feel the honour bestowed on an econometrician as an honour bestowed on all the econometricians who from 1930 on have tried to develop this science or this branch of science. It is very difficult indeed to find out who did what. There is only one thing that I would like to add personally.

There can be no doubt that Ragnar Frisch was the man who inspired us all in the annual meetings of the econometric society. If we had not had him, certainly econometrics would not have developed in the way it has developed. It is a great pity and a disappointment for us that he could not be here because he has broken his leg and I express the hope that soon he will be able to be here, as I understand is his plan. I would also like to join my colleagues in thanking all of you for the unforgettable days that my family and myself have had here in Stockholm. Thank you very much indeed.

JOHN R. HICKS
1972

INTRODUCTION

Sir John Richard Hicks (April 8, 1904 – May 20, 1989) was one of the most important and influential economists of the twentieth century.

His most influential contribution to the field of economics was the IS/LM model, which summarised the Keynesian view of macroeconomics. In 1972, Hicks was awarded the Nobel Prize in Economics together with Kenneth Arrow. He was born in 1904 at Warwick, England. He was educated at Clifton College (1917-22) and at Balliol College, Oxford (1922-26), an expensive education financed by mathematical scholarships. In 1923 he moved to "Philosophy, Politics and Economics", the "new school" just being started at Oxford; however he did not have adequate qualification in any of the subjects that he had studied. In 1935 he married Ursula Webb.

He spent the years from 1935 to 1938 at the University of Cambridge, mainly occupied with writing on his book Value and Capital. From 1938 to 1946 Hicks was a Professor at the Victoria University of Manchester. In 1946 he returned to Oxford, first being a research fellow of Nuffield College (1946-1965), then becoming Drummond Professor of Political Economy (1952-1965), and, after that, research fellow of All Souls College (1965-1971). In 1972 he shared the Nobel Prize with Kenneth J. Arrow.

PRIZE ACCEPTANCE SPEECH

John R. Hicks' speech at the Nobel Banquet in Stockholm, December 10, 1972

Mr. Prime Minister, Ladies and Gentlemen,

Economics comes in at the end; that (I am sure) is where we belong. Our science colleagues find permanent truths; economists, who deal with the daily actions of men and the consequences of these actions, can rarely hope to find the same permanency. There are parts of economics which are firmer than others, in this respect; to these parts Kenneth Arrow and I have made, I think, our contributions. But these parts are concerned with constraints on human aspiration; why we cannot do all we would like to do, even why we cannot do all we think we ought to do. Economics, at our end, if it is the more scientific end, is also the more uncomfortable end. I cannot therefore help feeling - even now - surprised that we are here. I think of the words of the Roman historian "rara temporum felicitate" - the mere moment of history, in which he felt himself to be living "when one may think what one chooses and say what one thinks". Like Tacitus, we enjoy a rare felicity - it's certainly that when practitioners of our uncomfortable science can receive a Prize of the hands of a Prince.

FRIEDRICH AUGUST VON HAYEK
1974

INTRODUCTION

In 1974 Friedrich von Hayek got the nobel price for his life activities in economy. Austrian-born British economist noted for his conservative views and criticisms of the Keynesian welfare state. In 1974 he shared the Nobel Prize for Economics with the Swedish economic liberal Gunnar Myrdal "for their pioneering work in the theory of money and economic fluctuations and for their penetrating analysis of the interdependence of economic, social and institutional phenomena"

Hayek studied law and psychology, then economics, at the University of Vienna, receiving a doctorate in 1923. After studying at New York University (1923-24), he became director of the Austrian Institute of Economic Research and then in 1931 moved to London, where he held positions at the University of London and the London School of Economics and Political Science.

In 1938 he became a naturalized British citizen. From 1950 to 1962 he was professor of social and moral science at the University of Chicago. Upon reaching retirement age, he accepted a chair at the University of Freiburg, retiring in 1968.

In 1944 he suggested in The Road to Serfdom that mild piecemeal reforms and governmental manipulations inevitably lead to the kind of ultimate domestic disaster that paves the way for totalitarian takeover by a Hitler. Hayek's other works include Prices and Production (1931), The Pure Theory of Capital (1941), The Constitution of Liberty (1960), Law,

Legislation, and Liberty (1978), and Unemployment and Monetary Policy: Government as Generator of the Business Cycle (1979).

PRIZE ACCEPTANCE SPEECH

Friedrich August von Hayek's speech at the Nobel Banquet, December 10, 1974

Your Majesty, Your Royal Highnesses, Ladies and Gentlemen,

Now that the Nobel Memorial Prize for economic science has been created, one can only be profoundly grateful for having been selected as one of its joint recipients, and the economists certainly have every reason for being grateful to the Swedish Riksbank for regarding their subject as worthy of this high honour.

Yet I must confess that if I had been consulted whether to establish a Nobel Prize in economics, I should have decidedly advised against it.

One reason was that I feared that such a prize, as I believe is true of the activities of some of the great scientific foundations, would tend to accentuate the swings of scientific fashion.

This apprehension the selection committee has brilliantly refuted by awarding the prize to one whose views are as unfashionable as mine are.

I do not yet feel equally reassured concerning my second cause of apprehension.

It is that the Nobel Prize confers on an individual an authority which in economics no man ought to possess.

This does not matter in the natural sciences. Here the influence exercised by an individual is chiefly an influence on his fellow experts; and they will soon cut him down to seize if he exceeds his competence.

But the influence of the economist that mainly matters is an influence over laymen: politicians, journalists, civil servants and the public generally.

There is no reason why a man who has made a distinctive

contribution to economic science should be omnicompetent on all problems of society - as the press tends to treat him till in the end he may himself be persuaded to believe.

One is even made to feel it a public duty to pronounce on problems to which one may not have devoted special attention.

I am not sure that it is desirable to strengthen the influence of a few individual economists by such a ceremonial and eye-catching recognition of achievements, perhaps of the distant past.

I am therefore almost inclined to suggest that you require from your laureates an oath of humility, a sort of hippocratic oath, never to exceed in public pronouncements the limits of their competence.

Or you ought at least, on confering the prize, remind the recipient of the sage counsel of one of the great men in our subject, Alfred Marshall, who wrote:

"Students of social science, must fear popular approval: Evil is with them when all men speak well of them".

MILTON FRIEDMAN
1976

INTRODUCTION

Milton Friedman (born July 31, 1912) is an American economist, known for his work on macroeconomics, microeconomics, economic history, statistics, and for his advocacy of laissez-faire capitalism.

In 1976, he won the Nobel Memorial Prize in Economics for his achievements in the fields of consumption analysis, monetary history and theory and for his demonstration of the complexity of stabilization policy.

In the late 1930s and again in 1941-43, Friedman worked for the federal government, becoming an advisor to high Treasury officials. As a spokesman for the U.S. Treasury in 1942 he advocated a Keynesian policy of taxation, and indeed helped develop the payroll withholding system of income tax payments.

Columbia University awarded him a Ph.D. in 1946. He then served as Professor of Economics at the University of Chicago, from 1946 to 1976, where he helped build a close-knit intellectual community that produced a number of Nobel Prize winners, known collectively as the Chicago School of Economics. Since 1977, Friedman has been affiliated with the Hoover Institution at Stanford University. Friedman also received National Medal of Science in 1988.

According to Harry Girvetz and Kenneth Minogue, Friedman is co-responsible with Friedrich von Hayek for providing the intellectual foundations for the revival of classical liberalism in the 20th century.

In 2005, Friedman and more than 500 other economists, called for discussions regarding the economic benefits of the legalization of marijuana.

PRIZE ACCEPTANCE SPEECH

Milton Friedman's speech at the Nobel Banquet, December 10, 1976

Your Majesties, Your Royal Highnesses, Ladies and Gentlemen,

It is a great honour and privilege for me to be here tonight, sharing in the reflected glory from my distinguished colleagues, not only the six fellow members of the class of 1976, but the many more who, over the past 76 years, have made the term Nobel Laureate the highest mark of distinction to which a scholar can aspire.

My science is a late-comer, the Prize in Economic Sciences in Memory of Alfred Nobel having been established only in 1968 by the Central Bank of Sweden to celebrate its tercentenary. That circumstance does, I admit, leave me with something of a conflict of interest. As some of you may know, my monetary studies have led me to the conclusion that central banks could profitably be replaced by computers geared to provide a steady rate of growth in the quantity of money. Fortunately for me personally, and for a select group of fellow economists, that conclusion has had no practical impact... else there would have been no Central Bank of Sweden to have established the award I am honoured to receive. Should I draw the moral that sometimes to fail is to succeed? Whether I do or not, I suspect some economists may.

Delighted as I am with the award, I must confess that the past eight weeks have impressed on me that not only is there no free lunch, there is no free prize. It is a tribute to the world-wide repute of the Nobel awards that the announcement of an award converts its recipient into an instant expert on all and sundry, and unleashes hordes of ravenous newsmen and photographers from journals and T.V. stations around the world. I myself have been asked my opinion on everything from a cure for the common cold to the market value of a letter signed by John F. Kennedy. Needless to say, the attention is flattering, but also corrupting. Somehow, we badly need an antidote for both the inflated attention granted a Nobel Laureate in areas outside his competence and the inflated ego each of us is in so much danger of acquiring. My own field suggests one obvious antidote: competition through the establishment of many more such awards. But a product that has been so successful is not easy to displace. Hence, I suspect that our inflated egos are safe for a good long time to come.

I am deeply grateful to you not only for the honor you have conferred on me, but equally for your unfailing Swedish hospitality and friendship.

SIR ARTHUR LEWIS
1979

INTRODUCTION

Sir William Arthur Lewis (January 23, 1915 – June 15, 1991) was a Saint Lucian economist well known for his contributions in the field of economic development.

In 1979 he won the Bank of Sweden Prize in Economic Sciences in Memory of Alfred Nobel, "for his pioneering research into economic development research with particular consideration of the problems of developing countries", also known as the Nobel Prize in Economics, becoming the first black person to win a Nobel Prize in a category other than peace.

Lewis was born in Saint Lucia, then still a British territory in the Caribbean. After gaining his BSc. in 1937 and Ph.D. in 1940 at the London School of Economics, Lewis lectured at the University of Manchester before being appointed Vice Chancellor of the University of the West Indies in 1959.

In 1963 he was both knighted and appointed a lecturer at Princeton University (a position in which he would remain until his retirement in 1983) and in 1970 became director of the Caribbean Development Bank. He died on June 15, 1991 in Bridgetown, Barbados and was buried in the grounds of the St Lucian community college named in his honour.

Lewis's Nobel prize-winning work consists of 2 models that describe and explain the problems facing developing nations.

PRIZE ACCEPTANCE SPEECH

Sir Arthur Lewis' speech at the Nobel Banquet, December 10, 1979

Your Majesties, Your Royal Highnesses, Ladies and Gentlemen,

The privilege of accepting the greetings of the students has been accorded to me, and I seize it gladly. On behalf of this year's laureates I say - Welcome fellow students, the path is hard, and we cannot see very far ahead of us, but the fellowship is wonderful.

I gladly seize the opportunity because it recognizes that tonight's laureates include two who were born and bred in the poorer parts of the world, that are now playing a larger part in world affairs. This Third World, as it is sometimes called, is experiencing revolutions of many kinds - political, economic, cultural - but none more fundamental than the scientific revolution, which is inherent in all the others. Science affects all our ways of thinking about the world, both the physical world which, if I may make so bold, is easy to understand because it is regular and follows simple laws, and also the social world, which is more baffling and less predictable.

Our countries are a couple of centuries late, and have a lot of catching up to do. We shall cross the same ground in a much shorter time. But it will not be exactly the same ground, not only in the sense that science throws off old skins as it grows, but also in the sense that geography alters the subject matter of some parts of science. This is obvious in relation to biology, or ecology, or economics, or sociology. But it applies even to physics, at the level of technology, where one can invent and choose between different ways of doing the same thing, some of which are more appropriate than others to the resources at hand. So we cannot in the Third World simply borrow or buy science from those ahead of us. Pure science we can take as it comes, but much of applied science we have to make for ourselves. Giant strides have been taken over the past thirty years inside the Third World, in building, equipping and managing new research institutes of every kind, and there is already a substantial pay-off.

Beyond such institutions, the strength of the scientific establishment in any country is related to its general level of education, not only in supplying large numbers of eager minds for further training, but also in ensuring a public opinion that holds science in esteem and approves financial support. Education is the great growth industry of the Third World. Since the second world war we have multiplied the number of children in school by four, with even larger multiples for secondary and university education. This is a turbulent process. We cannot give our students all that they expect, whether by way of the quality of their schooling, or by way of the jobs that they were hoping to get. Student frustration is a world wide phenomenon, pushing our societies into adjusting faster than they are used to.

I salute the student body of Sweden, and hope that its frustration will open up for it new and fruitful opportunities to serve the whole community.

RICHARD STONE
1984

INTRODUCTION

Sir John Richard Nicholas Stone British economist who in 1984 received the Nobel Prize for Economics "for having made fundamental contributions to the development of systems of national accounts and hence greatly improved the basis for empirical economic analysis". He is sometimes known as the father of national income accounting.

Stone initially studied law at the University of Cambridge, but, under the influence of economist John Maynard Keynes, he took a degree in economics in 1935 (Sc.D., 1957).

He worked for a brokerage firm in London (1936–40), and in 1940, at the invitation of Keynes, he entered the British government's Central Statistical Office. After World War II he was appointed director of the new department of applied economics at Cambridge.

He retained that position until 1955, when he became P.D. Leake professor of finance and accounting at Cambridge (1955–80; professor emeritus from 1980). He was knighted in 1978.

PRIZE ACCEPTANCE SPEECH

Richard Stone's speech at the Nobel Banquet, December 10, 1984

Your Majesties, Your Royal Highnesses, Ladies and Gentlemen,

Since the 18th of October I have been the prey to many emotions. First of all came surprise at having been selected for this high honour. Then came elation as the truth of it sank in. Then bewilderment at the Niagara of publicity that engulfed me. Then panic at the thought of producing a decent lecture in six weeks. Then exhilaration at the wonderful welcome I have received in Stockholm. Today, overshadowing them all is gratitude.

First, I want to thank the Nobel Foundation for making me feel like le Roi Soleil, a feeling which I am sure is shared by my fellow laureates.

Second, I want to thank my Swedish colleagues for singling me out for this year's Prize in Economics and the Royal Academy of Sciences for ratifying their choice. In so doing, they have given very great pleasure and encouragement not only to me but also to political arithmeticians, or, as we would say nowadays, economic statisticians, all over the world, as many of the letters I have received testify.

Third, I want to thank the Bank of Sweden for adding to the other Nobel prizes this one, which confirms incontrovertibly the standing of economics as a Science with a capital S.

Fourth, I want to thank the U.N. and the OECD for offering me soundboards of international resonance for my ideas.

Fifth, I want to thank the University of Cambridge for first giving me my education and then providing an ideal setting for my research.

Finally, I want to thank all the people who have written to me expressing, some seriously, some humorously, a degree of warmth and friendliness which I have found overwhelming.

I cannot conclude better than by quoting from one of these letters. But first I must explain that during the war, when I was working in the Central Statistical Office producing the first British national accounts, I always wrote with a quill pen - you know, one of those pens made out of a goose's feather. Well, my boss of those distant days, Sir Harry Campion, has not forgotten it. His charming letter of congratulations ends with the words: 'It just shows what can be done if you start with a quill pen and plenty of paper'.

ROBERT M. SOLOW
1987

INTRODUCTION

Robert Solow was born in Brooklyn, New York on August 23, 1924, the oldest of three children. He was well educated in the neighborhood public schools of New York City and excelled academically early in life. He was awarded the John Bates Clark Medal in 1961 and the Bank of Sweden Prize in Economic Sciences in Memory of Alfred Nobel ("Nobel Prize") in 1987 "for his contributions to the theory of economic growth".

In September 1940, Solow went to the Harvard College with a scholarship. At Harvard, his first studies were in sociology and anthropology as well as elementary economics.

By the end of 1942, Solow left the university and joined the U.S. Army. He served briefly in North Africa and Sicily, and later served in Italy during World War II until he was discharged in August 1945.

He returned to Harvard in 1945, and studied under Wassily Leontief. As his research assistant he produced the first set of capital-coefficients for the input-output model. Then he became interested in statistics and probability models.

In 1949, just before going off to Columbia he was offered and accepted an Assistant Professorship in the Economics Department at "Massachusetts Institute of Technology". At M.I.T. he taught courses in statistics and econometrics. Solow's interest gradually changed to Macroeconomics.

For almost 40 years, Solow and Paul Samuelson worked together on many landmark theories: von Neumann growth theory (1953), capital theory(1956), linear programming (1958) and the Phillips Curve (1960).

Solow also held several government positions, including senior economist for the Council of Economic Advisers (1961–62) and member of the President's Commission on Income Maintenance (1968–70). His studies focused mainly in the fields of employment and growth policies, and the theory of capital.

PRIZE ACCEPTANCE SPEECH

Robert M. Solow's speech at the Nobel Banquet, December 10, 1987

Your Majesties, Your Royal Highnesses, Ladies and Gentlemen:

Seven weeks have gone by since it became known that I had won this Prize. During that time I have been asked how to solve the economic problems of the United States, Norway, Sweden, the Federal Republic of Germany, Israel, Spain, Portugal, Argentina, Brazil, Mexico, the Philippines, China, Japan, and Korea. It goes without saying that I know the answers to all those questions, but it would be unfair to tell you the answers so soon. So I would like to talk about something else, not even about myself.

There must be very many people in this room, even in this room, who do not know that Sweden - this very small country with so few hours of daylight in winter - has a grand tradition in economics. It goes back beyond the beginning of this century with such great names as Knut Wicksell, David Davidsson and Gustav Cassel, and continues down to the present day. In the 1930s and 1940s and 1950s there was an astonishing renaissance of Swedish economics giving rise to what became famous around the world as the Stockholm School. There were no fewer than five celebrated names in economics: Erik Lindahl, Ingvar Svennilsson, Gunnar Myrdal, Bertil Ohlin, and Erik Lundberg. I want to mention them specifically because time passes and it is possible that I will be the last winner of this Prize to have known them all. There were other eminent members of the Stockholm School; I should mention, in this place, Dag Hammarskjöld, who is better known to you in other capacities.

I want most of all to say a word about my friend Erik Lundberg who died only three months ago. Erik Lundberg was both a great economist and a wonderful man. Only Erik Lundberg could have remarked, at the end of a conference on a very complicated problem, that he had been confused at the beginning of the conference, and, now that it was over, he felt confused at a higher level. His confusions were worth more than other people's certainties. I am sad not to see him here, because I know he would have been happy to see me standing in this place. Indeed I am happy to be standing in this place, and I wish to thank my colleagues of the Royal Swedish Academy of Sciences and to thank you all.

HARRY M. MARKOWITZ
1990

INTRODUCTION

Harry Max Markowitz (born August 24, 1927) is an influential economist at the Rady School of Management at the University of California, San Diego. Formerly at the RAND Corporation, Markowitz won the Bank of Sweden Prize in Economic Sciences in Memory of Alfred Nobel in 1990 "for his pioneering work in the theory of financial economics".

He is best known for his pioneering work in modern portfolio theory, studying the effects of asset risk, correlation and diversification on expected investment portfolio returns.

A Markowitz Efficient Portfolio is one where no added diversification can lower the portfolio's risk for a given return expectation (alternately, no additional expected return can be gained without increasing the risk of the portfolio).

The Markowitz Efficient Frontier is the set of all portfolios that will give the highest expected return for each given level of risk. These concepts of efficiency were essential to the development of the Capital Asset Pricing Model. Markowitz also co-edited the textbook The Theory and Practice of Investment Management with Frank J. Fabozzi of Yale School of Management.

PRIZE ACCEPTANCE SPEECH

Harry M. Markowitz' speech at the Nobel Banquet, December 10, 1990

Your Majesties, Your Royal Highnesses, Ladies and Gentlemen,

I would like to express my deepest thanks to the Nobel Foundation for the honor you do us, on behalf of the three of us who are here tonight and on behalf of hundreds of others who consider Financial Economics to be their principal field. We take this award to be a recognition and acceptance of Financial Economics as a branch of Economics, equal to any, as much as a reward for the efforts of three individuals.

At a more personal level I would like to thank Your Majesties, Your Royal Highnesses - indeed I would like to thank all of Sweden - for the great, grand good time you have shown my family and me during this wonderful Nobel week.

Many, many thanks to all of you. Thank you..

GARY S. BECKER
1992

INTRODUCTION

Gary Stanley Becker (born December 2, 1930) is an American economist. A professor at the University of Chicago, he won the 1992 Bank of Sweden Prize in Economic Sciences in Memory of Alfred Nobel for "having extended the domain of microeconomic analysis to a wide range of human behavior and interaction, including non-market behavior". He is also a member of the Hoover Institution and the National Bureau of Economic Research.

Born in Pottsville, Pennsylvania, he earned a B.A. at Princeton University in 1951 and a Ph.D. at the University of Chicago in 1955. He won the John Bates Clark Medal in 1967. Becker was one of the first economists to branch into what were traditionally considered topics belonging to sociology, including racial discrimination, crime, family organization, and drug addiction.

He is known for arguing that many different types of human behavior can be seen as rational and utility maximizing. His approach can include altruistic behavior by defining individuals' utility appropriately. He is also among the foremost exponents of the study of human capital. Becker is also credited with the "rotten kid theorem".

PRIZE ACCEPTANCE SPEECH

Gary S. Becker's speech at the Nobel Banquet, December 10, 1992

Your Majesties, Your Royal Highnesses, Ladies and Gentlemen,

I would like to express my gratitude to the Royal Swedish Academy of Sciences for the superb honor conferred on me. It is not necessary to have special reasons to be happy to be here, but I do feel especially pleased. This Prize gives recognition in the most influential way possible to all economists who endured many obstacles, criticisms, and even ridicule to study and analyze broader aspects of behavior than is traditional in economics.

During the first half of this century economics became more of a systematic science, but it also became increasingly isolated from the study of society, law and government. I was fortunate to have had outstanding teachers, several who later won this Prize. They supported my desire to use economic theory to try to understand discrimination against minorities and other questions that were much broader than those that had become the core of economics. I am grateful for their insights and encouragement.

I am not revealing any professional secrets when I state that not very long ago this type of research was not popular among most economists and other social scientists. But attitudes are changing, and there are now thriving schools of scholars in many fields using what is called the economic approach to analyze nonmarket and social behavior.

Economics is a very young science in comparison with the physical and biological sciences. Still, much is now known about economic and social life, although perhaps even more remains to be learned. For the economic and social world is mysterious, and it sometimes changes quickly and in surprising fashion. Every time we peel away some of the mystery, deeper challenges rise to the surface.

Economics surely does not provide a romantic vision of life. But the widespread poverty, misery, and crises in many parts of the world, much of it unnecessary, are strong reminders that understanding economic and social laws can make an enormous contribution to the welfare of people.

DOUGLASS C. NORTH
1993

INTRODUCTION

Douglass Cecil North (born November 5, 1920) is co-recipient of the 1993 Bank of Sweden Prize in Economic Sciences in Memory of Alfred Nobel "for having renewed research in economic history by applying economic theory and quantitative methods in order to explain economic and institutional change". He joined the faculty of Washington University in Saint Louis in 1983 as the Henry R. Luce Professor of Law and Liberty in the Department of Economics, and served as director of the Center for Political Economy from 1984 to 1990.

In 1992, he became the first economic historian ever to win one of the economics profession's most prestigious honors, the John R. Commons Award, which was established by the International Honors Society in Economics in 1965. Along with Ronald Coase and Oliver Williamson, he helped found the International Society for the New Institutional Economics which held its first meeting in St. Louis in 1997.

His current research includes property rights, transaction costs, and economic organization in history as well as economic development in developing countries.

Born in Cambridge, Massachusetts, he graduated from the University of California, Berkeley with a B.A. in General Curriculum-Humanities in 1942 and a Ph.D. in Economics in 1952, and joined the Merchant Marine during World War II. Prior to finishing his PhD, North had also been a semiprofessional photographer and had worked with Dorothea Lange as well as other notable photographers.

PRIZE ACCEPTANCE SPEECH

Douglass C. North's speech at the Nobel Banquet, December 10, 1993

Your Majesties, Your Royal Highnesses, Ladies and Gentlemen,

On behalf of my fellow economic historian and close friend Robert Fogel and myself, I would like to express our gratitude to the Royal Swedish Academy of Sciences for the immense honor bestowed on us today. This prize not only honors us but provides recognition to the field of economic history as an important and integral part of economics.

The result of more than thirty five years of the new economic history, or cliometrics, is not only to shed new light on the past as a result of the application of economic theory and quantitative methods to history but to provide social scientists with new insights into and a deeper understanding of the nature of societal and economic change. More than that, by developing new analytical tools to understand economic and social change economic historians are thereby adding important new dimensions to economics - and the other social sciences - attempting to confront the many economic and social problems of societies.

We have a long way to go in understanding the way economies and societies evolve through time; but the progress of the past three decades augurs well for the future. This award to economic historians will provide the recognition of our sub-discipline that will constitute an important spur for continued progress.

JAMES A. MIRRLEES
1996

INTRODUCTION

Professor Sir James Mirrlees, FBA (born July 5, 1936, Minnigaff, Scotland) is a Scottish economist and winner of the 1996 Bank of Sweden Prize in Economic Sciences in Memory of Alfred Nobel "for his fundamental contributions to the economic theory of incentives under asymmetric information". He was knighted in 1998.

He was educated at the University of Edinburgh and Trinity College, Cambridge, where he was a very active student debater. He taught at both Oxford (1969-1995) and Cambridge (1995-). It was during his time at Oxford that he published the economic models and equations for which he would eventually be awarded his Nobel Prize.

They centred around analysis of economic situations in which the information is asymmetrical or incomplete, determining the extent to which they should affect the optimal rate of saving in an economy.

Among other results, they demonstrated the principles of "moral hazard" and "optimal income taxation" discussed in the books of William Vickrey. The methodology has since become the standard in the field.

Vickrey and Mirrlees shared the 1996 Nobel Prize for Economics "for their fundamental contributions to the economic theory of incentives under asymmetric information". Mirrlees is emeritus Professor of Political Economy at the University of Cambridge, and a fellow of Trinity College, Cambridge. He spends several months a year at the University of Melbourne.

In 2006, he has been appointed as the Masters-Designate of the Morningside College of the Chinese University of Hong Kong.

PRIZE ACCEPTANCE SPEECH

James A. Mirrlees' speech at the Nobel Banquet, December 10, 1996

Majesties, Your Royal Highness, Ladies and Gentlemen,

The Nobel Prizes are about discovery and creation. It is the excitement of new discovery that they celebrate. It is wonderful to be a part of that celebration.

Economists are accustomed, perhaps surprisingly, to think about the world in terms of what I can only call proverbs. "There is no free lunch". This week has gone some way to disproving it. "Bygones are bygones". Apparently not: one's old work comes back now, and you encourage us to enjoy again what was once new. What proverbs, I wonder, are suggested by the work that Professor Vickrey and I have done? Perhaps, for a start, we have done a little to penetrate the "veil of ignorance".

Yet, corrupting some famous words, we might be felt to have shown that "One can tax all of the people some of the time; and some of the people all of the time; and if we put our minds to it, we can tax all of the people all of the time." The dismal science lives up to its reputation! Indeed, during these last few weeks, one of my former students, a Chinese economist, has been talking about my work in China. He has translated his version back from the Chinese: "Let the people tell the truth. Let the people work hard." It is amazing what becomes of discoveries once they are let loose in the world. You have been warned.

As you may know, according to economic theory, a prize once awarded should actually induce recipients to work less hard; and is therefore supposed to be not entirely good. But now I am of the opinion that, in the words of a Cambridge colleague, it is not entirely bad either. Thank you.

AMARTYA SEN
1998

INTRODUCTION

Dr Amartya Kumar Sen CH (Hon) (Bengali: Ômorto Kumar Shen) (born November 3, 1933 in India), is an economist and a winner of the Bank of Sweden Prize in Economic Sciences (sometimes referred to informally as the "Nobel Prize for Economics") in 1998, for his work on famine, human development theory, welfare economics, the underlying mechanisms of poverty, and political liberalism.

Sen was born in Santiniketan, West Bengal, the University town established by the poet Rabindranath Tagore, another Indian Nobel Prize winner. His ancestral home was in Wari, Dhaka in modern-day Bangladesh. Tagore is said to have given Amartya Sen his name ("Amartya" meaning "immortal"). Teaching that grades were not as important as creativity, Tagore helped to mold the intellectual diversity of young Sen.

Sen first studied in India at the school system of Visva-Bharati University, Presidency College, Kolkata and at the Delhi School of Economics before moving to Trinity College, Cambridge, where he earned a First Class BA in 1956 and then a Ph.D. in 1959. He was also allowed four years to immerse himself in philosophical issues during his stay at Trinity College.

He has taught economics at University of Calcutta, Jadavpur University, Delhi, Oxford (where he was the Drummond Professor of Political Economy and a Fellow of All Souls College), London School of Economics, Harvard and was Master of Trinity College, Cambridge, between 1998 and 2004.

In January 2004 Sen returned to Harvard. He is also a contributor to the Eva Colorni Trust at the former London Guildhall University, which has one of the best Economics Departments in the country.

PRIZE ACCEPTANCE SPEECH

Amartya Sen's speech at the Nobel Banquet, December 10, 1998

Your Majesties, Your Royal Highness, Ladies and Gentlemen,

More than two millennia ago, the poet Horace said, "It is lovely to be silly at the right moment." Well, I plead silliness in taking this to be the right moment.

Here is my first silly thought. Disciplinary boundaries can generate giddy suspicions. Physicists can receive post-modern criticism. Biologists took a long time to shake off the creationists. Economists and social scientists are, of course, especially suspect. W.H. Auden gave eloquent expression to this scepticism:

Thou shall not sit
With statisticians nor *commit*
A social science.

Well, we are reconciled to going on "committing" social science, sitting in our lonely corner, but it is nice to be able to see what the others are up to, on an occasion like this remarkable celebration of science and culture.

In fact, I am privileged to have known, as a child, the great Bengali poet, Rabindranath Tagore, who received the Nobel Prize in literature in 1913, and whose achievements include, among many other things, the authorship of the national anthems of two different countries - India and Bangladesh. Tagore had set up an unusual school in Santiniketan, where my grandfather was teaching; I was born on the school grounds. The school aimed at offering education that was at once local and global. As Tagore put it: "Whatever we understand and enjoy in human products instantly becomes ours, wherever they might have their origin." His universalist, tolerant and rationalist ideals were a strong influence on my thinking, and I often recollect them in these divisive times.

I believe that Chandrashekhar, the astrophysicist, who also originated in India, when he received his Nobel Prize in Physics, quoted a poem of Tagore, in praise of freedom of the mind: "where the clear stream of reason has not lost its way into the dreary desert sand of dead habit." Let me praise Chandrashekhar's praising of Tagore's praising the freedom of the mind.

Now a seriously silly thought. From this focus on open-minded reasoning, there is much that economists too can learn. The subject stands to lose a lot from dogmatic beliefs of one kind or another (for example, we are constantly asked: "Are you *against* or *in favour* of the market? *Against* or *in favour* of state action? Just answer the question - no qualifications, no 'ifs' and 'buts,' please!"). This is an invitation to replace analysis by slogans - to be guided by grand dogma, either of one kind, or of another. We do need "the clear stream of reason." What Tagore, the poet, and Chandrashekhar, the physicist, demanded, we need in economics too - for much the same reason. That is the last silly thought I inflict on you tonight.

DANIEL L. MCFADDEN
2000

INTRODUCTION

Daniel L. McFadden (born July 29, 1937) is an econometrician who won (jointly with James Heckman) the 2000 Bank of Sweden Prize in Economic Sciences in Memory of Alfred Nobel "for his development of theory and methods for analyzing discrete choice". He is currently the E. Morris Cox Professor of Economics at the University of California, Berkeley. McFadden was born in Raleigh, North Carolina.

After studying physics (B.S., 1957) and economics (Ph.D., 1962) at the University of Minnesota, McFadden taught economics at a number of institutions, including the University of California, Berkeley (1963–79), Yale University (1977–78), and the Massachusetts Institute of Technology (1978–91). In 1990 he returned to Berkeley and was named the E. Morris Cox Professor of Economics.

He also served (1991–95, 1996–) as the director of the university's Econometrics Laboratory. The recipient of numerous awards, McFadden was given the John Bates Clark Medal by the American Economics Association in 1975 and was elected to the National Academy of Sciences in 1981.

McFadden's work combined economic theory, statistical methods, and empirical applications toward the resolution of social problems. In 1974 he developed conditional logit analysis—a method for determining how individuals will choose among finite alternatives in order to maximize their utility.

Through the analysis of discrete choice (i.e., the choices made among a finite set of decision alternatives), McFadden's work helped predict usage rates for public transportation systems, and his statistical methods were applied to studies of labour-force participation, health care, housing (particularly for the elderly), and the environment.

PRIZE ACCEPTANCE SPEECH

Daniel L. McFadden's speech at the Nobel Banquet, December 10, 2000

Your Majesties, Your Royal Highnesses, Ladies and Gentlemen,

The term "economics", in its original Greek, means "of the hearth", the ancient and practical science of household management. Over the millennia, the discipline has transformed itself into a grander enterprise, speaking sagely of the organization of economies, and admonishing capitalists and kings on incentives, constraints, and unintended consequences. This is important business, but economists have felt the loss of their practical side. In the words of John Maynard Keynes, "If economists could manage to get themselves thought of as humble, competent people, on a level with dentists, that would be splendid!".

I think of the public edifice of economics as being like the inflatable buildings that cover tennis courts in cold climates, entirely supported by air. Yet, the air has a direction and purpose, and is the result of carefully designed and systematically maintained mechanical equipment that provides stability and form. It is at this practical, mechanical level, closer to the hearth than to the throne, that the science is put into economic science. Measurements are taken, designs are tested, and new machines are constructed.

Jim Heckman and I are engineers who build and operate machines that explain how people make choices, and how they select themselves into groups. Our machines are crafted with mathematics and live in computers, so they do not fire the public imagination like a new bridge or a new particle accelerator. However, in each case an innovative design can advance the science. Whether it is a well-written novel, a well-made wine, a fine dish, a clever computer chip, or a well-crafted microeconometric analysis, good design instructs, brings pleasure, and lifts the human spirit.

In light of the occasion and this season, and in the language of our subject, Jim Heckman and I offer you the following salutation: May you all select yourselves into the group that advances the welfare of humankind. May all your choices be discrete.

GEORGE A. AKERLOF
2001

INTRODUCTION

George Arthur Akerlof (born June 17, 1940) is an American economist and Koshland Professor of Economics at the University of California, Berkeley.

He won the Bank of Sweden Prize in Economic Sciences in Memory of Alfred Nobel in 2001 (shared with Michael Spence and Joseph E. Stiglitz) "for their analyses of markets with asymmetric information". His father was Swedish and his mother a Jewish American.

Akerlof is perhaps best known for his article, "The Market for Lemons: Quality Uncertainty and the Market Mechanism", published in Quarterly Journal of Economics in 1970, in which he identified the severe problems that may afflict markets characterized by asymmetrical information.

In Efficiency Wage Models of the Labor Market, Akerlof and coauthor Janet Yellen propose rationales for the efficiency wage hypothesis in which employers pay above the market-clearing wage, in contradiction to the conclusions of neoclassical economics.

Akerlof graduated from the Lawrenceville School and received his Bachelor's degree from Yale University in 1962, and his Ph.D. from MIT in 1966 and has taught at London School of Economics. His maternal great-grandfather was born in Oakland, California and was an alumnus of UC Berkeley (Class of 1873).

His maternal grandfather was also a Berkeley alumnus. His wife Janet Yellen is president of the Federal Reserve Bank of

San Francisco and a professor of economics at UC Berkeley and served on President Bill Clinton's Council of Economic Advisors.

PRIZE ACCEPTANCE SPEECH

George A. Akerlof 's speech at the Nobel Banquet, December 10, 2001

My colleagues and I would like to express our deepest gratitude for the prize bestowed upon us for our work on asymmetric information.

Asymmetric information occurs where buyers and sellers have different information.It has been present since the dawn of trade.

In this century we are careful in buying a used car.

In past centuries it would have been a horse.

Here are some of the tricks of the horse trader.

Bring a sad old nag to market.Put a live eel down her throat. She will be frisky.

Bring a high strung stallion to the ring.Give him a bucket of beer.He will be mellow.

These are the tricks.On one side of the market are the tricksters.The other side avoids the tricksters.

In the extreme, markets totally collapse.

And the good may lose out as well as the bad.

And so, it is difficult for the individual elderly to buy medical insurance, because those willing to pay high premia are presumed to be sick. And so, it is difficult for young people to attain credit to pursue their ideas, because the true will be mixed with the false.

This is the stuff that markets are made of:

How to sort the good from the bad.

In exploring such problems economists have gained an understanding of what is needed to make markets work.

We understand a pivotal piece of the puzzle why some

countries are poor while others are rich.

And we can work for the cure of the poverty that causes hunger, disease, and lives spent more in misery than in self-fulfillment for much of the globe.

At the time of our original papers, the exploration of asymmetric information was the next item on the agenda of the economics profession.

It is the achievement of a community of scholars each learning from one another, and then passing it on.

We accept the prizes you have given us in that spirit.

Little by little, step by step, women and men of ideas across the centuries and across the continents have wrested from nature a greater understanding of ourselves and also of God's creation.

Let that endeavor continue.

VERNON L. SMITH
2002

INTRODUCTION

Vernon Lomax Smith (born January 1, 1927 in Wichita, Kansas) is professor of economics and law at George Mason University and the George Mason University School of Law, a research scholar in the Interdisciplinary Center for Economic Science, and a Fellow of the Mercatus Center all in Arlington, Virginia.

An alumnus of Wichita North High School and Friends University, Smith received his bachelor's degree in electrical engineering from Caltech in 1949, an M.A. in economics from the University of Kansas in 1952, and his Ph.D. in economics from Harvard University in 1955.

Smith's first teaching post was at the Krannert School of Purdue University, which he held from 1955 until 1967, attaining the rank of full professor. It was there that his work in experimental economics began. As Smith describes it:

"In the Autumn semester, 1955, I taught Principles of Economics, and found it a challenge to convey basic microeconomic theory to students.

Smith also taught as a visiting associate professor at Stanford University (1961-1962) and there made contact with Sydney Siegel, who was also doing work in experimental economics. Smith moved with his family to Massachusetts and got a position first at Brown University (1967-1968), then at the University of Massachusetts (1968-1972). Smith also received appointments at the Center for Advanced Study in the Behavioral Sciences (1972-1973) and Caltech (1974-1975).

He moved on to the University of Arizona from 1976 until 2002, where he conducted research that earned him the Bank of Sweden Prize in Economic Sciences. He has authored or co-authored over 200 articles and books on capital theory, finance, natural resource economics and experimental economics.

Smith received the Bank of Sweden Prize in Economic Sciences in Memory of Alfred Nobel in 2002 "for having established laboratory experiments as a tool in empirical economic analysis, especially in the study of alternative market mechanisms". He served as an expert for the Copenhagen Consensus.

In February 2005 Smith spoke out publicly about his Asperger's syndrome, which is part of the autistic spectrum.

PRIZE ACCEPTANCE SPEECH

Vernon L. Smith's speech at the Nobel Banquet, December 10, 2002

I wish to celebrate:

- The Royal Family for their grace and charm in this magnificent affirmation of the dignity of humankind.
- Daniel Kahneman for his ingenuity in the study and understanding of human decision and its associated cognitive processes demonstrating that the logic of choice and the ecology of choice can be divergent.
- The pioneering influence of Sidney Siegel, Amos Tversky, Martin Shubik, and Charles Plott on the intellectual movement that culminated in the economics award for 2002.
- Humanity's most significant emergent creation: markets.
- Mandeville who said: "The worst of all the multitude did something for the common good."
- The ancient Judeo Commandments: Thou shalt not steal or covet the possessions of thy neighbor, which provide the property right foundations for markets, and warned that petty distributional jealousy must not be

allowed to destroy them. Neither shalt thou commit murder, adultery or bear false witness, which provide the foundations for cohesive social exchange.

- David Hume who declared the three laws of human nature: The right of possession, its transference by consent, and the performance of promises, and taught that the rules of morality are not the conclusions of reason.

- F.A. Hayek for teaching us that an economist who is only an economist cannot be a good economist; that fruitful social science must be very largely a study of what is not; that reason properly used recognizes its own limitations; that civilization rests on the fact that we all benefit from knowledge that we do not possess (as individuals).

- Benjamin Franklin who said "Tell me and I forget, teach me and I remember, involve me and I learn."

- And to Kahlil Gibran who reminds us that work is love made visible.

CLIVE W.J. GRANGER
2003

INTRODUCTION

Professor Sir Clive William John Granger (born September 4, 1934) is a Welsh-born economist, and Professor Emeritus at the University of California at San Diego, USA. Along with Robert Engle of New York University he shared the 2003 Bank of Sweden Prize in Economic Sciences in Memory of Alfred Nobel "for methods of analyzing economic time series with common trends (cointegration)".

He was born in Swansea, Wales, and educated at the University of Nottingham, England where he was an undergraduate and postgraduate student, and subsequently became a full professor. In all, he spent 22 years at the University before leaving for UCSD in 1974.

In 2005, the building that houses the Economics and Geography Departments at the University of Nottingham was renamed the Sir Clive Granger Building in honour of his Nobel achievement. Sir Clive Granger is married to Lady Patricia, and has two children, Mark and Claire.

He has said that the Norwegian economy is the best in the world. He was knighted in the 2005 New Year's Honours. He teaches for 2 months a year at the University of Melbourne, Australia.

PRIZE ACCEPTANCE SPEECH

Clive W.J. Granger's speech at the Nobel Banquet, December 10, 2003

Rob Engle and I are concerned with extracting useful implications from economic data, and so the properties of the data are of particular importance. Rob deals with financial markets which produce a virtually continuous stream of high quality data. He has available many time series which are strings of numbers plotted out through time.

I work with the macro economy, which involves the major variables that measure the health of the whole economy, such as total consumption, investment, income, employment, and inflation. These variables are measured monthly, or possibly quarterly (or even annually for a few countries).

The stock market is like a small row boat on a rough sea, bouncing around as it drifts, whereas the macro economy is like a large ocean liner, very ponderous and difficult to maneuver but without such a rough journey.

Because our data has different properties, Rob Engle and I developed different techniques to study our data, although there were some common foundations. Rob was concerned with quantifying the concept of risk in financial data and developed a very successful way of doing that, which he denoted ARCH. This measures the size of the waves or the bounce in stock market prices. I was more concerned with building models that central bankers could use for policy purposes and particularly for long run forecasting. The idea is called "cointegration" and provides ways to discover that two large boats are drifting with the same current or that two macroeconomies are moving together. You will find both of these words defined in the Oxford English Dictionary in a few years time!

Forecasts vary in horizon, from a few seconds up to a few days in financial markets, compared to from one to several months for macro variables. We have to provide uncertainty intervals around the central forecasts to indicate the extent to which we are unclear about the future. The ARCH models are concerned with variations in the confidence intervals at different horizons while my methods are concerned with coordination of forecasts for several variables.

The advantage that I have is that it may take a year or more to show that my forecasts were wrong, whereas Rob's could be found incorrect in about a day! Economists have a bad reputation for forecasting, but by using ARCH and Cointegration we can put forecasts and our confidence in their accuracy on a more scientific basis. These methods are now widely in place in business, government and academic research, and we thank the Nobel committee for its confidence in our forecasts.

Thank you.

EDWARD C. PRESCOTT
2004

INTRODUCTION

Edward C. Prescott, born 26 December 1940 in Glens Falls, New York, received the Nobel Memorial Prize in Economics in 2004, sharing the award with Finn E. Kydland, "for their contributions to dynamic macroeconomics: the time consistency of economic policy and the driving forces behind business cycles". This research was primarily conducted while both Kydland and Prescott were affiliated with the Graduate School of Industrial Administration at Carnegie Mellon University.

Currently working as an economist at the Federal Reserve Bank of Minneapolis and a Professor at Arizona State University's W.P. Carey School of Business, he is a major figure in macroeconomics, especially the theories of business cycles and general equilibrium.

In 1962, Prescott received his bachelor's degree in mathematics from Swarthmore College, where he was a member of the Delta Upsilon fraternity. He then received a master's degree from Case Western Reserve University in 1963 and a Ph.D. at Carnegie Mellon University in 1967. From 1966 to 1971, he taught at the University of Pennsylvania.

He then returned to Carnegie Mellon until 1980, when he moved to the University of Minnesota. In 1978, he was a visiting professor at the University of Chicago, where he was named a Ford Foundation Research Professor. In the following year, he visited Northwestern University and stayed there until 1982. Since 2003, he has been teaching at Arizona State. Currently, he is the Shinshei Bank Visiting Professor at New York University.

PRIZE ACCEPTANCE SPEECH

Edward C. Prescott's speech at the Nobel Banquet, December 10, 2004

Your Majesties, Your Royal Highnesses, Ladies and Gentlemen,

One of the great joys of research - whether it be in economics, physics, chemistry or any academic discipline - is the act of discovery, those moments when we are surprised by what we have found ... when our original ideas are turned upside down and we suddenly have to rearrange how we view the world.

This is precisely what happened to Finn and me when we were working on the two papers for which we have received this award. We were operating on previously held assumptions - just doing what we always had done and expecting similar results, when theory suddenly slapped us in the face and commanded us to pay attention. After the initial shock we humbly said, "Yes, Master," and we promptly changed our views.

You would think that we would have learned something from those experiences, but it happened to us again ... on three additional occasions! And each time it was immensely gratifying.

It is typical at events such as this to acknowledge the people who have influenced you and who have laid the foundation for your work, but there are far too many names and too little time to do justice to such a list. However, Finn, a Norwegian, said it would be okay if I mention the Swedes, who continue to have more than their fair share of people advancing the economic science. There is one Swede in particular, the great Knut Wicksell, whose work 100 years ago still has a major influence on how we conduct our science. And just to keep Finn happy I suppose I should mention one of the many marvelous Norwegian economists - Ragnar Frisch, who did so much to advance Wicksell's work.

But the people I would really like to acknowledge and celebrate are the students. They may not realize it now, but they are making history with their research and they will be the future Nobel Laureates. Their sense of wonder is a continual source of inspiration and never fails to energize me.

Some of those students will stand in this beautiful banquet hall some day and tell their own stories about how theory knocked some sense into them. I know it has knocked a lot of sense into me, and I look forward to many more such surprise discoveries.

Thank you very much.

ROBERT J. AUMANN
2005

INTRODUCTION

Yisrael Robert John Aumann (born June 8, 1930) is an Israeli mathematician and a member of the United States National Academy of Sciences. He works at the Center for the Study of Rationality in the Hebrew University of Jerusalem in Israel.

Aumann was awarded the 2005 Nobel Memorial Prize in Economics for "having enhanced our under-standing of conflict and cooperation through game-theory analysis". He shared the prize with Thomas Schelling.

The following press release from the Royal Swedish Academy of Sciences describes Aumann's work: In many real-world situations, cooperation may be easier to sustain in a long-term relationship than in a single encounter. Analyses of short-run games are, thus, often too restrictive. Robert Aumann was the first to conduct a full-fledged formal analysis of so-called infinitely repeated games. His research identified exactly what outcomes can be upheld over time in long-run relations.

The theory of repeated games enhances our understanding of the prerequisites for cooperation: Why it is more difficult when there are many participants, when they interact infrequently, when interaction is likely to be broken off, when the time horizon is short or when others' actions cannot be clearly observed. Insights into these issues help explain economic conflicts such as price wars and trade wars, as well as why some communities are more successful than others in managing common-pool resources.

The repeated-games approach clarifies the raison d'être of many institutions, ranging from merchant guilds and organized crime to wage negotiations and international trade agreements.

PRIZE ACCEPTANCE SPEECH

Robert J. Aumann's speech at the Nobel Banquet, December 10, 2005

Blessed are you, God, our Lord, Monarch of the Universe, who is good and does good.

After partaking of a meal with fine wines, we recite this benediction when we are served with a superb wine.

Your Royal Highnesses, we have, over the years, partaken of many fine wines. We have participated in the scientific enterprise: studied and taught, preserved, and pushed forward the boundaries of knowledge.

We have participated in the human enterprise " raised beautiful families. And I have participated in the realization of a 2000-year-old dream" the return of my people to Jerusalem, to its homeland.

And tonight, we have been served with a superb wine, in the recognition of the worth of our scientific enterprise.

I feel very strongly that this recognition is not only for us, but for all of game theory, in Israel and in the whole world "teachers, students, colleagues, and co-workers. And especially for one individual, who is no longer with us" the mother of game theory, Oskar Morgenstern.

So, I offer my thanks to these, to the Nobel Foundation and the Nobel Committee, to our magnificent hosts, the country of Sweden, and to the Lord, who is good and does good.

EDMUND S. PHELPS
2006

INTRODUCTION

Edmund Phelps was born in 1933 near Chicago, but he grew up and spent his school years in Hastings-on-Hudson, New York, where his family had moved when he was six years old. In 1951, he went to Amherst College as an undergraduate student.

After receiving his B.A. at Amherst in 1955, Phelps went to Yale University for graduate studies. Phelps received his Ph.D. from Yale in 1959. After receiving his Ph.D., Phelps went to work as an economist for the RAND Corporation. However, feeling that he could not pursue his main research interest, macroeconomics, at RAND (which focused on defense work), Phelps decided to return to the academic world. So, the next year, in 1960, he took a research position at the Cowles Foundation, while also doing some teaching at Yale.

In 1966, Phelps left Yale and moved to University of Pennsylvania, where he was offered a tenured position as professor of economics. In January 1969, Phelps organised at Penn a conference in support of the research on the microfoundations of inflation and employment determination. Phelps spent the year 1969-1970 at the Center for Advanced Study in Behavioral Science at Stanford University.

In 1971, Phelps moved to the Economics Department at Columbia University, which also included future Nobel prize winners William Vickrey and James J. Heckman (future laureate Robert Mundell joined three years later), as well as

Phoebus Dhrymes, Guillermo Calvo and John B. Taylor.

In 1990 Phelps took part in a mission from the then-forming EBRD to Moskow, where he and Kenneth Arrow designed a proposal for the reformal of the USSR. After the EBRD was established, he became a member of its Economic Advisory Board, where he stayed until 1993.

PRIZE ACCEPTANCE SPEECH

Edmund S. Phelps' speech at the Nobel Banquet, December 10, 2006

Your Majesties, Your Royal Highnesses, Ladies and Gentlemen

When I was a teenager I learned to play the trumpet. Music became my passion. Then, when I was in college at Amherst, my father asked me a favor: to take one course in economics. I loved it – for the challenge of its mysteries. I became as passionate about economics as I was about music. The economist Paul Samuelson became an idol alongside the trumpet man Harry James.

That passion gave me the drive to pursue a couple of the biggest remaining problems in economics. I took risks – tried to hit home runs.

In my graduate study at Yale I got a good start. My teachers included non-Keynesians as well as Keynesians, Europeans as well as Americans - Fellner, Koopmans, Triffin, Wallich, Tobin and Schelling. I acquired the diverse background I would need to do my research.

I didn't do my work for money or prizes – only for the excitement of discovery.

In my research, my best discovery was my wife Viviana! We have a beautiful life.

I've lived to see key parts of my research absorbed in textbooks and in central banks around the world. And some finance ministries too.

This award of the Prize in Economics in Memory of Alfred Nobel is an extremely public recognition by a most respected institution of some of my contributions. I am deeply grateful to the Royal Swedish Academy of Sciences and to its Nominating Committee for this wonderful honor.

ERIC S. MASKIN
2007

INTRODUCTION

Eric Stark Maskin (born December 12, 1950) is a American economist and co-winner, along with Leonid Hurwicz and Roger Myerson, of the 2007 Nobel Prize in Economics "for having laid the foundations of mechanism design theory."

He was born into a Jewish family and attended Harvard University where he received his A.B. and Ph.D. After he earned his doctorate from Harvard University, Eric went to the University of Cambridge in 1976 where he was a research fellow at Jesus College. He taught at MIT from 1977-1984 and from 1985-2000 at Harvard, where he was the Louis Berkman Professor of Economics. In 2000, he moved to the Institute for Advanced Study.

He has worked in diverse areas of economic theory, such as game theory, the economics of incentives, and contract theory. His current research projects include comparing different electoral rules, examining the causes of inequality and studying coalition formation. He is a Fellow of the *American Academy of Arts and Sciences, Econometric Society*, and the *European Economic Association*, and a Corresponding Fellow of the *British Academy*. He was president of the *Econometric Society* in 2003.

PRIZE ACCEPTANCE SPEECH

Eric S. Maskin's speech at the Nobel Banquet, 10 December 2007

Your Majesties, Your Royal Highnesses, Ladies and Gentlemen:

Robert Kennedy once said, "Some men see things as they are and ask why. I dream of things that never were and ask why not."

Those words reveal a deep truth about Kennedy: he was an *economist* at heart – startling though that may seem. In effect, the first line – seeing things as they are and asking why – perfectly describes *positive* economics, which explains economic events that have happened, or, better yet, forecasts what *will* happen. Economic forecasting has actually got pretty good over the years, though admittedly we don't always get it right. As one cynic noted, economists have predicted 9 out of the last 5 recessions. So, we take consolation from another great statesman, Yogi Berra, who observed that prediction is really hard – especially about the future.

Still, it is Kennedy's *second* line – dreaming of things that never were – that I want to stress, because it captures the part of economics dearest to me: *normative* economics, the study of the things that never were but *ought* to be. In particular, it describes the subject of this year's Economics Prize, mechanism design. Leo Hurwicz pioneered this subject nearly 50 years ago, and it has played a role in some of the most important economic policies of our time.

But two months ago scarcely anyone but economists had even heard of mechanism design. Suddenly, it has notoriety worthy of an Elvis Presley. Now, I have nothing against Elvis. But somehow he manages to attract a huge public following without even trying. Indeed, he can't very well try since he's been dead for 30 years. Yet, isn't it remarkable that, for one week a year, that kind of attention is focused not just on economics, but on physics, chemistry, medicine, and literature. And for that astounding accomplishment, I'd like to express my warmest appreciation to the Nobel Foundation and the Nobel awarding bodies.

Thank you.

LITERATURE

RABINDRANATH TAGORE
1913

INTRODUCTION

Indian author and guru, Calcutta. Tagore came from a wealthy Bengali family. He went abroad in 1877 to study law in England but soon returned to India. For a time he managed his father's estates and became involved with the Indian nationalist movement, writing propaganda. His characteristic later style combines natural des-criptions with religious and philosophical speculation.

Tagore drew on the classical literature of India, especially the ancient Sanskrit scriptures and the writings of Kalidasa. His prodigious output includes approximately 50 dramas, 100 books of verse (much of which he set to music), 40 volumes of novels and shorter fiction, and books of essays and philosophy.

In his devotion to peace, Tagore denounced nationalism and violence. He sought to instill in human beings a sense of their unity; he was severely critical of the Indian caste system. His most important philosophical work is *Sadhana: The Realization of Life* (1913), which echoes the fundamental ideas inherent in sacred Hindu writings. His dramas are filled with lyricism and philosophy, while his poems deal with amorous, mystical, and fabulous themes. In India his appeal was nearly universal. A man of striking appearance, Tagore came to be regarded with the reverence due an ancient teacher. He wrote in Bengali but translated much of his work into English. It attracted attention in the West, and he was awarded the 1913 Nobel Prize in Literature, especially for his collection of poetry, *Gitanjali* (1912). His *Janaganamana* (*Thou Art the Ruler of All Minds*) was adopted as the Indian national anthem.

Tagore's best-known novels and poetry include *The Gardener* (1913), *The Crescent Moon* (1913), *Songs of Kabir* (1915), *Cycle of Spring* (1917), *Fireflies* (1928), and *Sheaves* (1932). Among his plays are *The Post Office* (1914), *Chitra* (1917), and *Red Oleanders* (1924). Philosophical works include *Personality* (1917), *Nationalism* (1917), *The Home and the World* (1919), *The Religion of Man* (1931), and *Man* (1932). In 1915 Tagore was knighted. His travels and lectures took him around the world. He was impressed with the capacity of the West for accomplishing its practical goals, but he deprecated what he considered its spiritual emptiness and waste. In 1922, Santiniketan (abode of peace), the school he had founded at Bolpur in 1901, was expanded into the internationally attended Visva-Bharati Univ. The curriculum stressed social reform, international unity, and rural reconstruction.

PRIZE ACCEPTANCE SPEECH

Telegram from Rabindranath Tagore, read by Mr. Clive, British Chargé d'Affaires, at the Nobel Banquet at Grand Hôtel, Stockholm, December 10, 1913

I beg to convey to the Swedish Academy my grateful appreciation of the breadth of understanding which has brought the distant near, and has made a stranger a brother.

I AM glad that I have been able to come at last to your country and that I may use this opportunity for expressing my gratitude to you for the honour you have done to me by acknowledging my work and rewarding me by giving me the Nobel Prize.

I remember the afternoon when I received the cablegram from my publisher in England that the prize had been awarded to me. I was staying then at the school Shantiniketan, about which I suppose you know. At that moment we were taking a party over to a forest near by the school, and when I was passing by the telegram office and the post office, a man came running to us and held up the telegraphic message. I had also an English visitor with me in the same carriage. I did not think that the message was of any importance, and I just put it into my pocket, thinking that I would read it, when I reached my destination. But my visitor supposed he knew the contents, and he urged me to read it, saying that it contained an important message. And I opened and read the message, which I could hardly believe. I first thought that possibly the telegraphic language was not quite correct and that I might misread the meaning of it, but at last I felt certain about it. And you can well understand how rejoicing it was for my boys at the school and for the teachers. What touched me more deeply than anything else was that these boys who loved me and for whom I had the deepest love felt proud of the honour that had been awarded to him for whom they had feeling of reverence, and I realized that my countrymen would share with me the honour which had been awarded to myself.

The rest of the afternoon passed away in this manner, and when the night came I sat upon the terrace alone, and I asked myself the question what the reason could be of my poems being accepted and honoured by the West — in spite of my belonging to a different race, parted and separated by seas and mountains from the children of the West And I can assure you that it was not with a feeling of exaltation but with a searching of the heart that I questioned myself, and I felt humble at that moment.

I remember how my life's work developed from the time when I was very young. When I was about 25 years I used to live in utmost seclusion in the solitude of an obscure Bengal village by the river Ganges in a boat- house. The wild ducks which came during the time of autumn from the Himalayan lakes were my only living companions, and in that solitude I seem to have drunk in the open space like wine overflowing with sunshine, and the murmur of the river used to speak to me and tell me the secrets of nature. And I passed my days in the solitude dreaming and giving shape to my dream in poems and studies and sending out my thoughts to the Calcutta public through the magazines and other papers. You can well understand that it was a life quite different from the life of the West. I do not know if any of your Western poets or writers do pass the greatest part of their young days in such absolute seclusion. I am almost certain that it cannot be possible and that seclusion itself has no place in the Western world.

And my life went on like this. I was an obscure individual — to most of my countrymen in those days. I mean that my name was hardly known outside my own province, but I was quite content with that obscurity, which protected me from the curiosity of the crowds.

And then came a time when my heart felt a longing to come out of that solitude and to do some work for my human fellow-beings, and not merely give shapes to my dreams and meditate deeply on the problems of life, but try to give expression to my ideas through some definite work, some definitive service for my fellow-beings.

And the one thing, the one work which came to my mind was to teach children. It was not because I was specially fitted for this work of teaching, for I have not had myself the full benefit of a regular education. For some time I hesitated to take upon myself this task, but I felt that as I had a deep love for nature I had naturally love for children also. My object in starting this institution was to give the children of men full freedom of joy, of life and of communion with nature. I myself had suffered when I was young through the impediments which were inflicted upon most boys while they attended school and I have had to go through the machine of education which crushes the joy and freedom of life for which children have such insatiable thirst. And my object was to give freedom and joy to children of men.

And so I had a few boys around me, and I taught them, and I tried to make them happy. I was their playmate. I was their companion. I shared their life, and I felt that I was the biggest child of the party. And we all grew up together in this atmosphere of freedom. The vigour and the joy of the children, their chats and songs filled the air with a spirit of delight, which I drank every day I was there. And in the evening during the sun-set hour I often used to sit alone watching the trees of the shadowing avenue, and in the silence of the afternoon I could hear distinctly the voices of the children coming up in the air, and it seemed to me that these shouts and songs and glad voices were like those trees, which come out from the heart of the earth like fountains of life towards the bosom of the infinite sky. And it symbolized, it brought before my mind the whole cry of human life all expressions of joy and aspirations of men rising from the heart of Humanity up to this sky. I could see that, and I knew that we also, the grown-up children, send up our cries of aspiration to the Infinite. I felt it in my heart of hearts.

In this atmosphere and in this environment I used to write my poems Gitanjali, and I sang them to myself in the midnight under the glorious stars of the Indian sky. And in the early morning and in the afternoon glow of sun-set I used to write these songs till a day came when I felt impelled to come out once again and meet the heart of the large world.

I could see that my coming out from the seclusion of my life among these joyful children and doing my service to my fellow creatures was only a prelude to my pilgrimage to a larger world. And I felt a great desire to come out and come into touch with the Humanity of the West, for I was conscious that the present age belongs to the Western man with his superabundance of energy.

He has got the power of the whole world, and his life is overflowing all boundaries and is sending out its message to the great future. And I felt that I must before I die come to the West and meet the man of the secret shrine where the Divine presence has his dwelling, his temple. And I thought that the Divine man with all his powers and aspirations of life is dwelling in the West.

And so I came out. After my Gitanjali poems had been written in Bengali I translated those poems into English, without having any desire to have them published, being diffident of my mastery of that language, but I had — the manuscript with me when I came out to the West. And you know that the British public, when these poems were put before them, and those who had the opportunity of reading them in manuscript before, approved of them. I was accepted, and the heart of the West opened without delay.

And it was a miracle to me who had lived for fifty years far away from activity, far away from the West, that I should be almost in a moment accepted by the West as one of its own poets. It was surprising to me, but I felt that possibly this had its deeper significance and that those years which I had spent in seclusion, separated from the life and the spirit of the West, had brought with them a deeper feeling of rest, serenity and feeling of the eternal, and that these were exactly the sentiments that were needed by the Western people with their overactive life, who still in their heart of hearts have a thirst for the peace, for the infinite peace. My fitness was that training which my muse had from my young days in the absolute solitude of the beaches of the Ganges.

The peace of those years had been stored in my nature so that I could bring it out and hold it up to the man of the West, and what I offered to him was accepted gratefully.

I know that I must not accept that praise as my individual share. It is the East in me which gave to the West. For is not the East the mother of spiritual Humanity and does not the West, do not the children of the West amidst their games and plays when they get hurt, when they get famished and hungry, turn their face to that serene mother, the East Do they not expect their food to come from her, and their rest for the night when they are tired? And are they to be disappointed.

Fortunately for me I came in that very moment when the West had turned her face again to the East and was seeking for some nourishment. Because I represented the East I got my reward from my Eastern friends.

And I can assure you that the prize which you have awarded to me was not wasted upon myself. I as an individual had no right to accept it, and therefore I have made use of it for others. I have dedicated it to our Eastern children and students. But then it is like a seed which is put into the earth and comes up again to those who have sown it, and for their benefit it is producing fruits. I have used this money which I got from you for establishing and maintaining the university which I started lately, and it seemed to me, that this university should be a place where Western students might come and meet their Eastern brethren and when they might work together in the pursuit of truth and try to find the treasures that have lain hidden in the East for centuries and work out the spiritual resources of the East, which are necessary for all Humanity.

I can remind you of a day when India had her great university in the glorious days of her civilization. When a light is lighted it can not be held within a short range. It is for the whole world. And India had her civilization with all its splendours and wisdom and wealth. It could not use it for its own children only. It had to open its gates in hospitality to all races of men. Chinese and Japanese and Persians and all different races of men, came, and they had their opportunity of gaining what was best in India, her best offering of all times and to all Humanity. And she offered it generously. You know the traditions of our country are never to accept any material fees from the students in return to the teaching, because we consider in India that he who has the knowledge has the responsibility to impart it to the students. It is not merely for the students to come and ask it from the master, but it is the master who must fulfil his mission of life by offering the best gift which he has to all who may need it And thus it was that need of self-expression, of giving what had been stored in India and offering the best thing that she has in herself that made it possible and was the cause and the origin of these universities that were started in the different provinces of India.

And I feel that what we suffer from in the present day is no other calamity but this calamity of obscurity, of seclusion, that we have missed our opportunity of offering hospitality to Humanity and asking the world to share the best things we have got. We lost our confidence in our own civilization for over a century, when we came into contact with the Western races with their material superiority over the Eastern Humanity and Eastern culture, and in the educational establishments no provision was made for our own culture. And for over a century our students have been brought up in utter ignorance of the worth of their own civilization of the past. Thus we did not only lose touch of the great which lay hidden in our own inheritance, but also the great honour of being able to contribute to the civilization of Humanity, to have opportunity of giving what we have and not merely begging from others, not merely borrowing culture and living like eternal schoolboys.

But the time has come when we must not waste such our opportunities. We must try to do our best to bring out what we have, and not go from century to century, from land to land and display our poverty before others. We know what we have to be proud of, what we have inherited from our ancestors, and such opportunity of giving should not be lost — not only for the sake of our people, but for the sake of Humanity.

That is the reason, and that led me to the determination to establish an international institution where the Western and Eastern students could meet and share the common feast of spiritual food.

And thus I am proud to say that your awarding me the prize has made some contribution to this great object which I had in my mind. This has made me come out once again to the West, and I have come to ask you, to invite you to the feast which is waiting for you in the far East. I hope that my invitation will not be rejected. I have visited different countries of Europe, and I have accepted from them an enthusiastic welcome. That welcome has its own meaning, that the West has need of the East, as the East has need of the West, and so the time has come when they should meet.

I am glad that I belong to this great time, this great age, and I am glad that I have done some work to give expression to this great age, when the East and the West are coming together. They are proceeding towards each other. They are coming to meet each other. They have got their invitation to meet each other and join hands in building up a new civilization and the great culture of the future.

I feel certain that through my writing some such idea has reached you, even if obscurely through the translation, some idea which belongs both to the East and the West, some idea which proceeding from the East has been able to come to the West and claim its rest here, its dwelling, and to be able to receive its welcome, and has been accepted by the West. And if in my writings I have been fortunate enough to be able to interpret the voice of the need of the time I am deeply thankful to you for giving me this glorious opportunity. The acknowledgment I got from Sweden has brought me and my work before the Western public, though I can assure you that it has also given me some trouble. It has broken through the seclusion which I have been accustomed to. It has brought me out before the great public to which I have never been accustomed. And the adjustment has not been yet made. I shrink in my heart when I stand before the great concourse of Humanity in the West. I have not yet been accustomed to accept the great gift of your praise and your admiration in the manner in which you have given it to me. And I feel ashamed and shy when standing before you — I do so now. But I will only say that I am thankful to God that he has given me this great opportunity, that I have been an instrument to bring together, to unite the hearts of the East and the West. And I must to the end of my life carry on that mission. I must do all that I can. The feeling of resentment between the East and the West must be pacified. I must do something, and with that one object I have started this institution.

I do not think that it is the spirit of India to reject anything, reject any race, reject any culture. The spirit of India has always proclaimed the ideal of unity. This ideal of unity never rejects anything, any race, or any culture. It comprehends all, and it has been the highest aim of our spiritual exertion to be able to penetrate all things with one soul, to comprehend all things as they are, and not to keep out anything in the whole universe — to comprehend all things with sympathy and love. This is the spirit of India. Now, when in the present time of political unrest the children of the same great India cry for rejection of the West I feel hurt. I feel that it is a lesson which they have received from the west. Such is not our mission. India is there to unite all human races. Because of that reason in India we have not been given the unity of races. Our problem is the race problem which is the problem of all Humanity. We have Dravidians, we have Mohammedans, we have Hindoos and all different sects and communities of men in India. Therefore, no superficial bond of political unity can appeal to us, can satisfy us, can ever be real to us. We must go deeper down. We must discover the most profound unity, the spiritual unity between the different races. We must go deeper down to the spirit of man and find out the great bond of unity, which is to be found in all human races. And for that we are well equipped. We have inherited the immortal works of our ancestors, those great writers who proclaimed the religion of unity and sympathy, in say: He who sees all beings as himself, who realizes all beings as himself, knows Truth. That has once again to be realized, not only by the children of the East but also by the children of the West. They also have to be reminded of these great immortal truths. Man is not to fight with other human races, other human individuals, but his work is to bring about reconciliation and Peace and to restore the bonds of friendship and love. We are not like fighting beasts. It is the life of self which is predominating in our life, the self which is creating the seclusion, giving rise to sufferings, to jealousy and hatred, to political and commercial competition. All these illusions will vanish, if we go down to the heart of the shrine, to the love and unity of all races. For that great mission of India I have started this university. I ask you now, when I have this opportunity, I invite you to come to us and join hands with us and not to leave this institution merely to us, but let your own students and learned men come to us and help us to make this university to a common institution for the East and the West may they give the contributions of their lives and may we all together make it living and representative of the undivided Humanity of the world.

For this I have come to you. I ask you this and I claim it of you in the name of the unity of men, and in the name of love, and in the name of God. I ask you to come. I invite you.

WILLIAM BUTLER YEATS
1923

INTRODUCTION

William Butler Yeats was born in Dublin. His father was a lawyer and a well-known portrait painter. Yeats was educated in London and in Dublin, but he spent his summers in the west of Ireland in the family's summer house at Connaught. The young Yeats was very much part of the *fin de siècle* in London; at the same time he was active in societies that attempted an Irish literary revival. His first volume of verse appeared in 1887, but in his earlier period his dramatic production outweighed his poetry both in bulk and in import. Together with Lady Gregory he founded the Irish Theatre, which was to become the Abbey Theatre, and served as its chief playwright until the movement was joined by John Synge. His plays usually treat Irish legends; they also reflect his fascination with mysticism and spiritualism. *The Countess Cathleen* (1892), *The Land of Heart's Desire* (1894), *Cathleen ni Houlihan* (1902), *The King's Threshold* (1904), and *Deirdre* (1907) are among the best known.

After 1910, Yeats's dramatic art took a sharp turn toward a highly poetical, static, and esoteric style. His later plays were written for small audiences; they experiment with masks, dance, and music, and were profoundly influenced by the Japanese Noh plays. Although a convinced patriot, Yeats deplored the hatred and the bigotry of the Nationalist movement, and his poetry is full of moving protests against it. He was appointed to the Irish Senate in 1922. Yeats is one of the few writers whose greatest works were written after the award of the Nobel Prize. Whereas he received the Prize chiefly for his dramatic works, his significance today rests on his lyric achievement.

His poetry, especially the volumes *The Wild Swans at Coole* (1919), *Michael Robartes and the Dancer* (1921), *The Tower* (1928), *The Winding Stair and Other Poems* (1933), and *Last Poems and Plays* (1940), made him one of the outstanding and most influential twentieth-century poets writing in English. His recurrent themes are the contrast of art and life, masks, cyclical theories of life (the symbol of the winding stairs), and the ideal of beauty and ceremony contrasting with the hubbub of modern life.

He was awarded the Nobel Prize for Literature in 1923.

PRIZE ACCEPTANCE SPEECH

William Butler Yeats's speech at the Nobel Banquet at Grand Hôtel, Stockholm, December 10, 1923.

I have been all my working life indebted to the Scandinavian nation. When I was a very young man, I spent several years writing in collaboration with a friend the first interpretation of the philosophy of the English poet Blake. Blake was first a disciple of your great Swedenborg and then in violent revolt and then half in revolt, half in discipleship. My friend and I were constantly driven to Swedenborg for an interpretation of some obscure passage, for Blake is always in his mystical writings extravagant, paradoxical, obscure. Yet he has had upon the last forty years of English imaginative thought the influence which Coleridge had upon the preceding forty; and he is always in his poetry, often in his theories of painting, the interpreter or the antagonist of Swedenborg. Of recent years I have gone to Swedenborg for his own sake, and when I received your invitation to Stockholm, it was to his biography that I went for information. Nor do I think that our Irish theatre could have ever come into existence but for the theatre of Ibsen and Bjørnson. And now you have conferred upon me this great honour. Thirty years ago a number of Irish writers met together in societies and began a remorseless criticism of the literature of their country. It was their dream that by freeing it from provincialism they might win for it European recognition. I owe much to those men, still more to those who joined our movement a few years later, and when I return to Ireland these men and women, now growing old like myself, will see in this great honour a fulfilment of that dream. I in my heart know how little I might have deserved it if they had never existed.

Prior to Mr. Yeats's speech, Einar Lönnberg, President of the Academy of Sciences, addressed the Irish writer:

Mr. Yeats - A worthier tongue than mine has already given us a review of your literary work.

What more, then, can I do on this occasion than express our admiration and thank you for the beautiful visions you have revealed to us from the Emerald Isle? We have delighted in listening to the tales of the fairies and elves, with which you have made us acquainted. We have been especially charmed by your poem about the little "silver trout".

In another of your poems you have said:

"Time drops in decay
    Like a candle burnt out" - - -

It is true, but we should be happy if this day would remain long in your memory, as it certainly will in ours.

PEARL BUCK
1938

INTRODUCTION

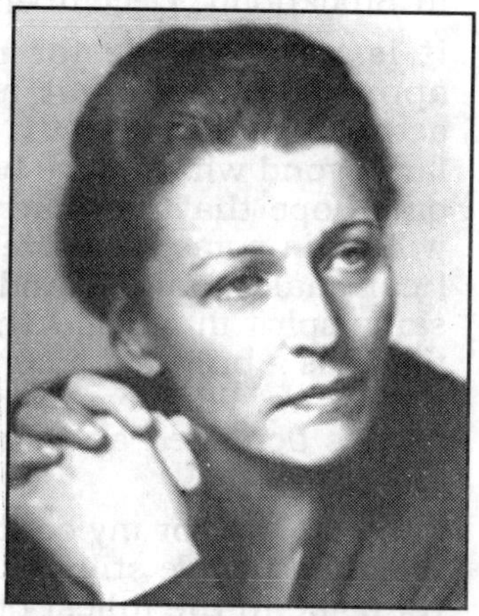

Pearl Buck (1892-1973) was born in Hillsboro, West Virginia. She grew up in China, where her parents were missionaries, but was educated at Randolph-Macon Woman's College. After her graduation she returned to China and lived there until 1934 with the exception of a year spent at Cornell University, where she took an M.A. in 1926. Pearl Buck began to write in the twenties; her first novel, *East Wind, West Wind*, appeared in 1930. It was followed by *The Good Earth* (1931), *Sons* (1932), and *A House Divided* (1935), together forming a trilogy on the saga of the family of Wang. *The Good Earth* stood on the American list of «best sellers» for a long time and earned her several awards, among them the Pulitzer Prize and the William Dean Howells Medal. She also published *The First Wife and Other Stories* (1933), *All Men are Brothers* (a translation of the Chinese novel *Shui Hu Chuan*) (1933), *The Mother* (1934), and *This Proud Heart* (1938). The biographies of her mother and father, *The Exile* and *Fighting Angel*, were published in 1936 and later brought out together under the title of *The Spirit and the Flesh* (1944). *The Time Is Now*, a fictionalized account of the author's emotional experiences, although written much earlier, did not appear in print until 1967.

Pearl Buck's works after 1938 are too many to mention. Her novels have continued to deal with the confrontation of East and West, her interest spreading to such countries as India and Korea. Her novelist's interest in the interplay of East and West has also led to some activity in political journalism.

Pearl Buck has been active in many welfare organizations; in particular she set up an agency for the adoption of Asian-American children (Welcome House, Inc.) and has taken an active interest in retarded children *(The Child Who Never Grew, 1950).*

PRIZE ACCEPTANCE SPEECH

Pearl Buck's speech at the Nobel Banquet at the City Hall in Stockholm, December 10, 1938

It is not possible for me to express all that I feel of appreciation for what has been said and given to me. I accept, for myself, with the conviction of having received far beyond what I have been able to give in my books. I can only hope that the many books which I have yet to write will be in some measure a worthier acknowledgment than I can make tonight. And, indeed, I can accept only in the same spirit in which I think this gift was originally given - that it is a prize not so much for what has been done, as for the future. Whatever I write in the future must, I think, be always benefited and strengthened when I remember this day.

I accept, too, for my country, the United States of America. We are a people still young and we know that we have not yet come to the fullest of our powers. This award, given to an American, strengthens not only one, but the whole body of American writers, who are encouraged and heartened by such generous recognition. And I should like to say, too, that in my country it is important that this award has been given to a woman. You who have already so recognized your own Selma Lagerlöf, and have long recognized women in other fields, cannot perhaps wholly understand what it means in many countries that it is a woman who stands here at this moment. But I speak not only for writers and for women, but for all Americans, for we all share in this.

I should not be truly myself if I did not, in my own wholly unofficial way, speak also of the people of China, whose life has for so many years been my life also, whose life, indeed, must always be a part of my life. The minds of my own country and of China, my foster country, are alike in many ways, but above all, alike in our common love of freedom.

And today more than ever, this is true, now when China's whole being is engaged in the greatest of all struggles, the struggle for freedom. I have never admired China more than I do now, when I see her uniting as she has never before, against the enemy who threatens her freedom. With this determination for freedom, which is in so profound a sense the essential quality in her nature, I know that she is *unconquerable*. Freedom - it is today more than ever the most precious human possession. We - Sweden and the United States - we have it still. My country is young - but it greets you with a peculiar fellowship, you whose earth is ancient and free.

HERMANN HESSE
1946

INTRODUCTION

German novelist and poet. A pacifist, he went to Switzerland at the outbreak of World War I and became (1923) a Swiss citizen. The spiritual loneliness of the artist and his es-trangement from the modern world are recurring themes in Hesse's works. His novels, increasingly psychoanalytic and symbolic, include *Peter Camenzind* (1904, tr. 1961), *Unterm Rad* (1906, tr. *Beneath the Wheel,* 1968), *Rosshalde* (1914, tr. 1970), and *Demian* (1919, tr. 1923, 1958). One of his most famous and most complex novels, *Steppenwolf* (1927, tr. 1929, 1963), treats the dual nature of humanity. This theme is also pursued in *Narziss und Goldmund* (1930, tr. *Death and the Lover,* 1932; *Narcissus and Goldmund,* 1968).

Among his other works are *Das Glasperlenspiel* (1943, tr. *The Glass Bead Game,* 1970) and *Siddhartha* (1922, tr. 1951), a novella reflecting Hesse's interest in Asian mysticism. The gentle, lyric quality of Hesse's prose is shared by the wistful, lamenting verse of his *Gedichte* (1922, tr. *Poems,* 1970) and *Trost der Nacht* (1929).

His essays are collected in *Betrachtungen* (1928) and *Krieg und Frieden* (1946, tr. *If the War Goes on... ,* 1970). Hesse was awarded the 1946 Nobel Prize in Literature.

PRIZE ACCEPTANCE SPEECH

As the Laureate was unable to be present at the Nobel Banquet at the City Hall in Stockholm, December 10, 1946, the speech was read by Henry Vallotton, Swiss Minister.

(Translation)

We deeply regret that illness keeps Hermann Hesse in Switzerland. But his thoughts are with us, and his gratitude speaks through this message which he asked me to read to you: "In sending cordial and respectful greetings to your festive gathering, I should like above all to express my regrets at not being able to be your guest in person, to greet and to thank you. My health has always been delicate, and I have been left a permanent invalid by the afflictions of the years since 1933 that have destroyed my life's work and have again and again burdened me with heavy duties. But my mind has not been broken, and I feel akin to you and to the idea that inspired the Nobel Foundation, the idea that the mind is international and supra-national, that it ought to serve not war and annihilation, but peace and reconciliation.

My ideal, however, is not the blurring of national characteristics, such as would lead to an intellectually uniform humanity. On the contrary, may diversity in all shapes and colours live long on this dear earth of ours. What a wonderful thing is the existence of many races, many peoples, many languages, and many varieties of attitude and outlook! If I feel hatred and irreconcilable enmity toward wars, conquests, and annexations, I do so for many reasons, but also because so many organically grown, highly individual, and richly differentiated achievements of human civilization have fallen victim to these dark powers. I hate the *grands simplificateurs*, and I love the sense of quality, of inimitable craftsmanship and uniqueness. As your grateful guest and colleague I therefore extend my greetings to Sweden, your country, to her language and civilization, her rich and proud history, and her perseverance in maintaining and shaping her individual nature. I have never been to Sweden, but for decades many a good and kind thing has come to me from your country since that first present which I received from it: it is now forty years ago and it was a Swedish book, a copy of the first edition of *Christ Legends* with a personal dedication by Selma Lagerlöf. In the course of years there has been many a valuable exchange with your country until you have now surprised me with the final great present. Let me express to you my profound gratitude."

SIR WINSTON CHURCHILL
1953

INTRODUCTION

The Right Honourable Sir Winston Leonard Spencer Churchill, the son of Lord Randolph Churchill and an American mother, was educated at Harrow and Sandhurst. After a brief but eventful career in the army, he became a Conservative Member of Parliament in 1900.

He held many high posts in Liberal and Conservative governments during the first three decades of the century. At the outbreak of the Second World War, he was appointed First Lord of the Admiralty - a post which he had earlier held from 1911 to 1915.

In May, 1940, he became Prime Minister and Minister of Defence and remained in office until 1945. He took over the premiership again in the Conservative victory of 1951 and resigned in 1955. However, he remained a Member of Parliament until the general election of 1964, when he did not seek re-election.

Queen Elizabeth II conferred on Churchill the dignity of Knighthood and invested him with the insignia of the Order of the Garter in 1953. Among the other countless honours and decorations he received, special mention should be made of the honorary citizenship of the United States which President Kennedy conferred on him in 1963.

Churchill's literary career began with campaign reports: *The Story of the Malakand Field Force* (1898) and *The River War* (1899), an account of the campaign in the Sudan and the Battle of Omdurman. In 1900, he published his only novel, *Savrola*, and, six years later, his first major work, the biography of his father,

Lord Randolph Churchill.

His other famous biography, the life of his great ancestor, the Duke of Marlborough, was published in four volumes between 1933 and 1938. Churchill's history of the First World War appeared in four volumes under the title of *The World Crisis* (1923-29); his memoirs of the Second World War ran to six volumes (1948-1953/54).

After his retirement from office, Churchill wrote a *History of the English-speaking Peoples* (4 vols., 1956-58). His magnificent oratory survives in a dozen volumes of speeches, among them *The Unrelenting Struggle* (1942), *The Dawn of Liberation* (1945), and Victory (1946).

Churchill, a gifted amateur painter, wrote *Painting as a Pastime* (1948). An autobiographical account of his youth, *My Early Life*, appeared in 1930.

He was awarded the Nobel Prize for Literature in 1953.

PRIZE ACCEPTANCE SPEECH

As the Laureate was unable to be present at the Nobel Banquet at the City Hall in Stockholm, December 10, 1953, the speech was read by Lady Churchill.

The Nobel Prize in Literature is an honour for me alike unique and unexpected and I grieve that my duties have not allowed me to receive it myself here in Stockholm from the hands of His Majesty your beloved and justly respected Sovereign. I am grateful that I am allowed to confide this task to my wife.

The roll on which my name has been inscribed represents much that is outstanding in the world's literature of the twentieth century. The judgment of the Swedish Academy is accepted as impartial, authoritative, and sincere throughout the civilized world. I am proud but also, I must admit, awestruck at your decision to include me. I do hope you are right. I feel we are both running a considerable risk and that I do not deserve it. But I shall have no misgivings if you have none.

Since Alfred Nobel died in 1896 we have entered an age of storm and tragedy. The power of man has grown in every sphere except over himself. Never in the field of action have events seemed so harshly to dwarf personalities. Rarely in history have brutal facts so dominated thought or has such a widespread, individual virtue found so dim a collective focus. The fearful question confronts us; have our problems got beyond our control? Undoubtedly we are passing through a phase where this may be so. Well may we humble ourselves, and seek for guidance and mercy.

We in Europe and the Western world, who have planned for health and social security, who have marvelled at the triumphs of medicine and science, and who have aimed at justice and freedom for all, have nevertheless been witnesses of famine, misery, cruelty, and destruction before which pale the deeds of Attila and Genghis Khan. And we who, first in the League of Nations, and now in the United Nations, have attempted to give an abiding foundation to the peace of which men have dreamed so long, have lived to see a world marred by cleavages and threatened by discords even graver and more violent than those which convulsed Europe after the fall of the Roman Empire.

It is upon this dark background that we can appreciate the majesty and hope which inspired the conception of Alfred Nobel. He has left behind him a bright and enduring beam of culture, of purpose, and of inspiration to a generation which stands in sore need. This world-famous institution points a true path for us to follow. Let us therefore confront the clatter and rigidity we see around us with tolerance, variety, and calm.

The world looks with admiration and indeed with comfort to Scandinavia, where three countries, without sacrificing their sovereignty, live united in their thought, in their economic practice, and in their healthy way of life. From such fountains new and brighter opportunities may come to all mankind. These are, I believe, the sentiments which may animate those whom the Nobel Foundation elects to honour, in the sure knowledge that they will thus be respecting the ideals and wishes of its illustrious founder.

ERNEST MILLER HEMINGWAY
1954

INTRODUCTION

Ernest Hemingway, born in Oak Park, Illinois, started his career as a writer in a newspaper office in Kansas City at the age of seventeen. After the United States entered the First World War, he joined a volunteer ambulance unit in the Italian army. Serving at the front, he was wounded, was decorated by the Italian Government, and spent considerable time in hospitals. After his return to the United States, he became a reporter for Canadian and American newspapers and was soon sent back to Europe to cover such events as the Greek Revolution.

During the twenties, Hemingway became a member of the group of expatriate Americans in Paris, which he described in his first important work, *The Sun Also Rises* (1926). Equally successful was *A Farewell to Arms* (1929), the study of an American ambulance officer's disillusionment in the war and his role as a deserter.

Hemingway used his experiences as a reporter during the civil war in Spain as the background for his most ambitious novel, *For Whom the Bell Tolls* (1940). Among his later works, the most outstanding is the short novel, *The Old Man and the Sea* (1952), the story of an old fisherman's journey, his long and lonely struggle with a fish and the sea, and his victory in defeat.

Hemingway - himself a great sportsman - liked to portray soldiers, hunters, bullfighters - tough, at times primitive people whose courage and honesty are set against the brutal ways of modern society, and who in this confrontation lose hope and faith. His straightforward prose, his spare dialogue, and his predilection for understatement are particularly effective in his short stories, some of which are collected in *Men Without Women* (1927) and *The Fifth Column and the First Forty-Nine Stories* (1938). Hemingway died in Idaho in 1961.

He was awarded the Nobel Prize for Literature in 1954.

PRIZE ACCEPTANCE SPEECH

As the Laureate was unable to be present at the Nobel Banquet at the City Hall in Stockholm, December 10, 1954, the speech was read by John C. Cabot, United States Ambassador.

Having no facility for speech-making and no command of oratory nor any domination of rhetoric, I wish to thank the administrators of the generosity of Alfred Nobel for this Prize.

No writer who knows the great writers who did not receive the Prize can accept it other than with humility. There is no need to list these writers. Everyone here may make his own list according to his knowledge and his conscience.

It would be impossible for me to ask the Ambassador of my country to read a speech in which a writer said all of the things which are in his heart. Things may not be immediately discernible in what a man writes, and in this sometimes he is fortunate; but eventually they are quite clear and by these and the degree of alchemy that he possesses he will endure or be forgotten.

Writing, at its best, is a lonely life. Organizations for writers palliate the writer's loneliness but I doubt if they improve his writing. He grows in public stature as he sheds his loneliness and often his work deteriorates. For he does his work alone and if he is a good enough writer he must face eternity, or the lack of it, each day.

For a true writer each book should be a new beginning where he tries again for something that is beyond attainment. He should always try for something that has never been done or that others have tried and failed. Then sometimes, with great luck, he will succeed.

How simple the writing of literature would be if it were only necessary to write in another way what has been well written. It is because we have had such great writers in the past that a writer is driven far out past where he can go, out to where no one can help him.

I have spoken too long for a writer. A writer should write what he has to say and not speak it. Again I thank you.

JOHN STEINBECK
1962

INTRODUCTION

American writer, b. Salinas, Calif., studied at Stanford. He is probably best remembered for his strong sociological novel *The Grapes of Wrath,* considered one of the great American novels of the 20th cent. Steinbeck's early novels—*Cup of Gold* (1929), *The Pastures of Heaven* (1932), and *To a God Unknown* (1933)—attracted little critical attention, but *Tortilla Flat* (1935), an affectionate yet realistic novel about the lovable, exotic, Spanish-speaking poor of Monterey, was enthusiastically received.

A compassionate understanding of the world's disinherited was to be Steinbeck's hallmark. The novel *In Dubious Battle* (1936) defends striking migrant agricultural workers in the California fields. In the novella *Of Mice and Men* (1937; later made into a play), Steinbeck again presents migrant workers, but this time in terms of human worth and integrity—a theme he also used in *The Moon Is Down* (1942; later made into a play), about Norwegian resistance to the Nazis.

The Grapes of Wrath (1939; Pulitzer Prize), while treating the plight of dispossessed Dust Bowl farmers during the 1930s, presents a universal picture of victims of disaster. Steinbeck's depiction of the westward migration of the Joad family, and their subsequent struggles in the exploitative agricultural industry of California, is realistic and moving, and he endows his humble characters with nobility.

Steinbeck's other works are diverse, ranging from the literal account of a voyage, *The Sea of Cortez* (1941; written with the marine biologist E. F. Ricketts); to a parable, *The Pearl* (1948); to a playful French folk piece, *The Short Reign of Pippin IV* (1957).

Love of his native land shines through the exquisitely nostalgic story "The Red Pony" in *The Long Valley* (1938). The somewhat sentimental attitude of *Tortilla Flat* appears again in *Cannery Row* (1945), *The Wayward Bus* (1947), and *Sweet Thursday* (1954). More ambitious are the novels *East of Eden* (1952), a family chronicle with the Cain and Abel theme, and *Winter of Our Discontent* (1961), about a suburbanite's moral conflict.

Steinbeck also wrote notable nonfiction, particularly *The Log from the Sea of Cortez* (1951) and *A Russian Journal* (1948), and the screenplays for the motion pictures *The Forgotten Village* (1941) and *Viva Zapata!* (1952).

Travels with Charley in Search of America appeared in 1962 and *America and Americans* in 1966. Steinbeck was awarded the 1962 Nobel Prize in Literature.

PRIZE ACCEPTANCE SPEECH

John Steinbeck's speech at the Nobel Banquet at the City Hall in Stockholm, December 10, 1962

I thank the Swedish Academy for finding my work worthy of this highest honor.

In my heart there may be doubt that I deserve the Nobel award over other men of letters whom I hold in respect and reverence - but there is no question of my pleasure and pride in having it for myself.

It is customary for the recipient of this award to offer personal or scholarly comment on the nature and the direction of literature. At this particular time, however, I think it would be well to consider the high duties and the responsibilities of the makers of literature.

Such is the prestige of the Nobel award and of this place where I stand that I am impelled, not to squeak like a grateful and apologetic mouse, but to roar like a lion out of pride in my profession and in the great and good men who have practiced it through the ages.

Literature was not promulgated by a pale and emasculated critical priesthood singing their litanies in empty churches - nor is it a game for the cloistered elect, the tinhorn mendicants of low calorie despair.

Literature is as old as speech. It grew out of human need for it, and it has not changed except to become more needed.

The skalds, the bards, the writers are not separate and exclusive. From the beginning, their functions, their duties, their responsibilities have been decreed by our species.

Humanity has been passing through a gray and desolate time of confusion. My great predecessor, William Faulkner, speaking here, referred to it as a tragedy of universal fear so long sustained that there were no longer problems of the spirit, so that only the human heart in conflict with itself seemed worth writing about.

Faulkner, more than most men, was aware of human strength as well as of human weakness. He knew that the understanding and the resolution of fear are a large part of the writer's reason for being.

This is not new. The ancient commission of the writer has not changed. He is charged with exposing our many grievous faults and failures, with dredging up to the light our dark and dangerous dreams for the purpose of improvement.

Furthermore, the writer is delegated to declare and to celebrate man's proven capacity for greatness of heart and spirit - for gallantry in defeat - for courage, compassion and love. In the endless war against weakness and despair, these are the bright rally-flags of hope and of emulation.

I hold that a writer who does not passionately believe in the perfectibility of man, has no dedication nor any membership in literature.

The present universal fear has been the result of a forward surge in our knowledge and manipulation of certain dangerous factors in the physical world.

It is true that other phases of understanding have not yet caught up with this great step, but there is no reason to presume that they cannot or will not draw abreast. Indeed it is a part of the writer's responsibility to make sure that they do.

With humanity's long proud history of standing firm against natural enemies, sometimes in the face of almost certain defeat and extinction, we would be cowardly and stupid to leave the field on the eve of our greatest potential victory.

Understandably, I have been reading the life of Alfred Nobel

- a solitary man, the books say, a thoughtful man. He perfected the release of explosive forces, capable of creative good or of destructive evil, but lacking choice, ungoverned by conscience or judgment.

Nobel saw some of the cruel and bloody misuses of his inventions. He may even have foreseen the end result of his probing - access to ultimate violence - to final destruction. Some say that he became cynical, but I do not believe this. I think he strove to invent a control, a safety valve. I think he found it finally only in the human mind and the human spirit. To me, his thinking is clearly indicated in the categories of these awards.

They are offered for increased and continuing knowledge of man and of his world - for understanding and communication, which are the functions of literature. And they are offered for demonstrations of the capacity for peace - the culmination of all the others.

Less than fifty years after his death, the door of nature was unlocked and we were offered the dreadful burden of choice.

We have usurped many of the powers we once ascribed to God.

Fearful and unprepared, we have assumed lordship over the life or death of the whole world - of all living things.

The danger and the glory and the choice rest finally in man. The test of his perfectibility is at hand.

Having taken Godlike power, we must seek in ourselves for the responsibility and the wisdom we once prayed some deity might have.

Man himself has become our greatest hazard and our only hope.

So that today, St. John the apostle may well be paraphrased: In the end is the Word, and the Word is Man - and the Word is with Men.

CZESLAW MILOSZ
1980

INTRODUCTION

Poet, essayist, and novelist, Szetejnie, Lithuania (then in Russia). Widely considered the greatest contemporary Polish poet, Milosz was born into an ethnically Polish family, studied law in Vilnius and literature in Paris, lived in Warsaw during World War II, joined (1946) the diplomatic service, and in 1951 gained political asylum from Communist Poland while he was a cultural attaché in France.

He lived in the United States from 1960, when he began teaching at the Univ. of California, Berkeley, until 1989, when he returned to a non-Communist Poland. He began writing verse in 1931, developing his own distinctive poetic voice some five years later. Although fluent in a number of languages, he wrote in his native Polish throughout his career. The main source of his early poetry was the Lithuanian countryside of his youth, which also figures prominently in his autobiographical novel *The Issa Valley* (1955, tr. 1981). Often tragic and ironic, his poetry was profoundly affected by World War II and, later, by the Communist dictatorship in Poland.

He has been characterized as a poet of exile, memory, and witness, and much of his mature verse and many of his essays are modest yet profound meditations on the fate of humanity and culture in a fallen world.

His best-known prose work, *The Captive Mind* (1953, tr. 1955), is an essay collection that studies the spiritual condition of society under Stalinist totalitarianism. He is also well known for the novel *The Seizure of Power* (tr. 1955) and the long poem

A Treatise on Poetry (1957, tr. 2001). Among his many other works are the classically styled verse of *Bells in Winter* (tr. 1978), *Provinces* (tr. 1991), *New and Collected Poems, 1931–2001* (tr. 2001), and the posthumously published *Second Space* (2004).

His work also includes *History of Polish Literature* (1969, 2d ed. 1983); and the essay collections *Emperor of the Earth* (1977), *Visions from San Francisco Bay* (tr. 1982), *The Witness of Poetry* (tr. 1983), and *Beginning with My Streets* (1985, tr. 1991).

He was awarded the Nobel Prize in Literature in 1980.

PRIZE ACCEPTANCE SPEECH

Czeslaw Milosz' speech at the Nobel Banquet, December 10, 1980

Your Majesty, Your Royal Highnesses, Ladies and Gentlemen,

I accept this highest honor on behalf of all men and women for whom I am not so much an individual as a voice, and someone who belongs to them. They should be invoked here, and they come from more than one country. First of all, I think of those who cherish the Polish language and literature, wherever they live, in Poland or abroad; I also think of my part of Europe, the nations situated between Germany and Russia, the nations in whose future of freedom and dignity I believe; and particularly my thoughts go to a country where I was born, Lithuania. Moreover, since I have lived a long time in exile, I may be legitimately claimed by all those who had to leave their native villages and provinces because of misery of persecution and to adapt themselves to new ways of life; we are millions all over the Earth, for this is a century of exile. Neither should I bypass here my new home country, America, where not only I found, as many before me, hospitality and well-rewarded work, but also the friendship of American poets. And though the University of California, where for twenty years I have been teaching Slavic Literatures, counts among its professors several Nobel Prize winners in science, today it is particularly pleased being able to add to their number its first Nobel laureate in humanities.

There is a paradox inherent in the poet's calling. Savagely individualistic, pursuing goals which are visible only to his few intimate friends, he grows accustomed to be branded as difficult and obscure, only to discover one day that his poems constitute a link between people and that he must assume, whether he wants it or not, a symbolic role. Living a long time abroad, I gradually became a poet of the young generations in Poland, and, as I guess, my adventure has some auspicious features of a general import. Poets and their readers may be separated by distance but if a spiritual unity between them is preserved, borders and barriers, thatever their nature, have not power. I think that we, both in Poland and outside, accomplished an important thing by refusing to recognize a division of Polish literature into two separate bodies, depending on where a given writer lives. Credit should here be given to those of my colleagues who have not been swayed by absurd doctrines, and to the young who have promoted free exchange of ideas, whether through lectures, periodicals or books. Volumes of my poetry published by their independent presses are most precious items on my bookshelves. No lesser homage is due to the astonishing energy and perseverance of a few persons who founded abroad institutions dedicated to publishing books and periodicals in Polish, such as the Literary Institute in France, that has been active without interruption since the end of the war and has been engaged in issuing books both of authors in exile and of those from Poland. Such a continuity and unity of a culture, maintained in most unfavorable circumstances, speaks against romantic moods of irrevocability and nostalgia, attached by the nineteenth century to the notion of exile.

I am a part of Polish literature which is relatively little known in the world as it is hardly translatable. Comparing it with other literatures, I have been able to appreciate its rich oddity. It is a kind of a secret brotherhood with its own rites of communion with the dead, where weeping and laughter, pathos and irony coexist on an equal footing, history-oriented, always allusive, in this century, as before, it faithfully accompanied the people in their hard trials. Lines of Polish verse circulated underground, were written in barracks of concentration camps and in soldiers' tents in Asia, Africa, and Europe. To represent here such a literature is to feel humble before testimonies of love and heroic selfsacrifice left by those who are no more. It is my hope that the distinction kindly granted to me by the Swedish Academy indirectly rewards all who guided my hand and whose invisible presence sustained me in difficult moments.

WILLIAM GOLDING
1983

INTRODUCTION

William Golding was born in Cornwall in 1911 and was educated at Marlborough Grammar School and at Brasenose College, Oxford. Apart from writing, his past and present occupations include being a schoolmaster, a lecturer, an actor, a sailor, and a musician. His father was a schoolmaster and his mother was a suffragette.

He was brought up to be a scientist, but revolted. After two years at Oxford he read English literature instead, and became devoted to Anglo-Saxon. He spent five years at Oxford. Published a volume of poems in 1935. Taught at Bishop Wordsworth's School, Salisbury. Joined the Royal Navy in 1940 and spent six years afloat, except for seven months in New York and six months helping Lord Cherwell at the Naval Research Establishment. He saw action against battleships (at the sinking of the Bismarck), submarines and aircraft. Finished as Lieutenant in command of a rocket ship.

He was present off the French coast for the D-Day invasion, and later at the island of Walcheren. After the war he returned to teaching, and began to write again. *Lord of the Flies*, his first novel, was published in 1954. It was filmed by Peter Brook in 1963.

In 1980 he won the 'Booker Prize' for his novel *Rites of Passage*. He retired from teaching in 1962. After that, he lived in Wiltshire, listing his recreations as music, sailing, archaeology and classical Greek.

William Golding died in 1993.

PRIZE ACCEPTANCE SPEECH

William Golding's speech at the Nobel Banquet, December 10, 1983

Your Majesties, your Royal Highnesses, your Excellencies, Fellow Laureates, Ladies and Gentlemen,

I came to Sweden characterized as a pessimist, though I am an optimist. Now something - perhaps the wonderful warmth of your hospitality - has changed me into a comic. That is a hard position to sustain. It reminds me of days long ago when as a poor teacher I would take turn about during the night with my wife, getting our infant daughter to sleep. I remember once, how at three o'clock in the morning when I began to creep away from the cradle with its sleeping child, she opened her eyes and remarked: "Daddy, say something funny"

However, the moment has come for me to put off the jester's cap and bells.

I do thank Sweden for its wonderfully warm hospitality and I do thank the Nobel Foundation and the Swedish Academy for the welcome and unexpected way in which they have, so to speak, struck me with lightning. I only wish all borders were as easy to cross and all international exchanges as friendly. I have been in many countries and I have found there people examining their own love of life, sense of peril, their own common sense. The one thing they cannot understand is why that same love of life, sense of peril and above all common sense, is not invariably shared among their leaders and rulers.

Then let me use what I suppose is my last minute of worldwide attention to speak not as one of a nation but as one of mankind. I use it to reach all men and women of power. Go back. Step back now. Agreement between you does not need cleverness, elaboration, manoeuvres. It needs common sense, and above all, a daring generosity. Give, give, give! It would succeed because it would meet with worldwide relief, acclaim and rejoicing: and unborn generations will bless your name.

JOSÉ SARAMAGO
1998

INTRODUCTION

Portuguese novelist and short-story writer. A Communist, Saramago was essentially a journalist until the revolution of 1974. Often employing paradox and irony and mingling humor with melancholy, much of his work provides a Portuguese view of Iberian history, blending historical events with mythical and allegorical elements.

Saramago's protagonists are often portrayed resisting some kind of stifling and dehumanizing social institution. His novels include *Levantado do chão* [raised from the floor] (1980); *Memorial do convento* (1982; tr. *Baltasar and Blimunda,* 1987), the work that first brought him international acclaim; *O ano da morte de Ricardo Reis* (1984; tr. *The Year of the Death of Ricardo Reis,* 1990); *A jangada de pedra* (1986; tr. *The Stone Raft,* 1995); *O evangelho segundo Jesus Cristo* (1991; tr. *The Gospel According to Jesus Christ,* 1994); *Ensaio sobre a cegueira* (1995; tr. *Blindness,* 1998), perhaps his finest work; *Todos os nomes* (1997; tr. *All the Names,* 1999); *A Caverna* (2000; tr. *The Cave,* 2002); and *Homem duplicado* (2002; tr. *The Double,* 2004). He has also written poetry, essays, plays, and a journal. Saramago was awarded the Nobel Prize in Literature in 1998.

PRIZE ACCEPTANCE SPEECH

José Saramago's speech at the Nobel Banquet, Dec. 10, 1998

Majesties, Royal Higness, Ladies and Gentlemen,

The Universal Declaration of Human Rights was signed today exactly 50 years ago. There is no lack of ceremonial commemorations. The attention fades, you know. When serious matters emerge the public interest starts to diminish, the next day even. I hold nothing against these commemorative acts. I myself have contributed to them, in my modest way, and if it is not out of place or time or ill-advised let me add some more. In this half-century, obviously governments have not morally done for human rights all that they should. The injustices multiply, the inequalities get worse, the ignorance grows, the misery expands. This same schizophrenic humanity that has the capacity to send instruments to a planet to study the composition of its rocks can with indifference note the deaths of millions of people from starvation. To go to Mars seems more easy than going to the neighbour. Nobody performs her or his duties. Governments do not, because they do not know, they are not able or they do not wish, or because they are not permitted by those who effectively govern the world: The multinational and pluricontinental companies whose power - absolutely non-democratic - reduce to next to nothing what is left of the ideal of democracy. We citizens are not fulfilling our duties either. Let us think that no human rights will exist without symmetry of the duties that correspond to them. It is not to be expected that governments in the next 50 years will do it. Let us common citizens therefore speak up. With the same vehemence as when we demanded our rights, let us demand responsibility over our duties. Perhaps the world could turn a little better.

I have not forgotten the thanks. In Frankfurt, on the 8th of October, my first words of thanks were for the Swedish Academy for granting me the Nobel Prize in Literature. I thanked as well my publishers, my translators and my readers. Again thank you all. And now also I wish to thank the Portuguese writers and writers in the Portuguese language, the ones of the past and of today: It is through them our literature exists. I am but one of them. I said that day that I was not born for this, but it was given to me. Thus, my best thanks.

V. S. NAIPAUL
2001

INTRODUCTION

English author, Chaguanas, Trinidad; grad. University College, Oxford, 1953. Naipul, whose family is descended from Indian Brahmins, has lived in England since 1950. A master of English prose style, he is known for his penetrating analyses of alienation and exile.

In fiction and essays marked by stylistic virtuosity and psychological insight, he often focuses on his childhood and his travels beyond Trinidad. Writing with increasing irony and pessimism, he has often bleakly detailed the dual problems of the Third World: the oppressions of colonialism and the chaos of postcolonialism.

Among Naipaul's works of international analysis are *The Middle Passage* (1962), about the West Indies and South America, and an Indian trilogy: *An Area of Darkness* (1964), *India: A Wounded Civilization* (1977), and *India: A Million Mutinies Now* (1990).

His novels include *The Mystic Masseur* (1957), *A House for Mr. Biswas* (1961), *In a Free State* (1971; Booker Prize), *Guerrillas* (1975), *A Bend in the River* (1979), and *Half a Life* (2001) and its sequel, *Magic Seeds* (2004); he has also written numerous short stories.

Among his other works are *The Enigma of Arrival* (1987) and *A Way in the World* (1994), autobiographical works combining novel, memoir, and history; *Among the Believers* (1981) and *Beyond Belief* (1998), analyses of modern Islam; and many political essays, a representative sample of which are collected in *The Writer and the World* (2002).

Naipaul was knighted in 1990 and awarded the Nobel Prize in Literature in 2001.

PRIZE ACCEPTANCE SPEECH

Sir V. S. Naipaul's speech at the Nobel Banquet, December 10, 2001

Your Majesties, Your Royal Highnesses, Honoured Laureates, Ladies and Gentlemen,

One of the things that happen to people who get the Nobel Prize is that they get a lot of media attention. Many interviews. So many that I begin to feel now that I have lost the capacity for spontaneous thought. I need the questions. So I thought I would begin this two-minute speech like the old-fashioned comedian.. The man to whom things happen on the way to the studio.

Well, then. Something happened to me on the way to Stockholm. The strap of my wrist-watch broke. And for some surreal moments I found myself looking at my watch on the floor of the plane. This is no metaphor. Here is the strapless watch. What did it mean? What was the awful symbolism? The fact that all through the Nobel week I was to be without my watch.

The great Caesar, landing in Egypt, fell flat on his face on the wet shore. You can imagine the consternation of his officers, until the great and resourceful man shouted, "Africa, I've got you!" Some centuries later, the Emperor Julian, training one morning with his soldiers, lost the wicker part of his shield. He was left holding only the grip or the handle. How terrible for everybody until the Emperor shouted, "What I have I hold".

Not having the resourcefulness of these great men, I could find no words to make the bad symbolism good. Until tonight, when I understood that time was to stop for me during this Nobel week, and that, when it began again, it would be truly new. Now my strapless watch, benign again, tells me without threat that my time is running out. My two minutes are up.

IMRE KERTÉSZ
2002

INTRODUCTION

Imre Kertész was born in Budapest on November 9, 1929. Of Jewish descent, in 1944 he was deported to Auschwitz and from there to Buchenwald, where he was liberated in 1945. On his return to Hungary he worked for a Budapest newspaper, *Világosság*, but was dismissed in 1951 when it adopted the Communist party line. After two years of military service he began supporting himself as an independent writer and translator of German-language authors such as Nietzsche, Hofmannsthal, Schnitzler, Freud, Roth, Wittgenstein, and Canetti, who have all had a significant influence on his own writing.

Kertész's first novel, *Sorstalanság* , a work based on his experiences in Auschwitz and Buchenwald, was published in 1975. "When I am thinking about a new novel, I always think of Auschwitz," he has said. This does not mean, however, that *Sorstalanság* is autobiographical in any simple sense: Kertész says himself that he has used the form of the autobiographical novel but that it is not autobiography. Sorstalanság was initially rejected for publication. When published eventually in 1975, it was received with compact silence. Kertész has written about this experience in *A kudarc* (1988; *Fiasco*).

This novel is normally regarded as the second volume in a trilogy that begins with *Sorstalanság* and concludes with *Kaddis a meg nem született gyermekért*, in a title that refers to the Jewish prayer for the dead.

In *Kaddis a meg nem született gyermekért*, the protagonist of *Sorstalanság* and *A kudarc*, György Köves, reappears. His Kaddish is said for the child he refuses to beget in a world that permitted the existence of Auschwitz. Other prose works are *A nyomkereso*" (1977; *The pathfinder*) and *Az angol labogó*.

Gályanapló, a diary in fictional form that covers the years 1961-91, was published in 1992. *Valaki más: A változás krónikája* (1997; *I - another: Chronicle of a metamorphosis*), continues this inner monologue in the form of notes made during the years 1991-95. After the political upheavals of 1989, Kertész was able to make more public appearances.

His lectures and essays have been collected in *A holocaust mint kultúra* (1993; *The holocaust as culture*), *A gondolatnyi csend, amíg kivegzo"oztag újratölt* (1998; *Moments of silence while the execution squad reloads*), and *A számu"ött nyelv* (2001; *The exiled language*).

Imre Kertész was awarded the Brandenburger Literaturpreis in 1995, the Leipziger Buchpreis zur Europäischen Verständigung in 1997, the Herder- Preis and the WELT-Literaturpreis in 2000, the Ehrenpreis der Robert-Bosch-Stiftung in 2001, and the Hans Sahl-Preis in 2002.

His works have been translated into numerous languages, including German, Spanish, French, English, Czech, Russian, Swedish, and Hebrew.

In 2002 he was awarded the Nobel Prize in Literature.

PRIZE ACCEPTANCE SPEECH

Imre Kertész's speech at the Nobel Banquet, December 10, 2002

Today we are experiencing a globalization, an inflation of the Holocaust. The Holocaust survivor who knows Auschwitz through the experience of suffering, observes it all from the perspective assigned to him. He keeps silent or gives interviews to the Spielberg Foundation, he accepts the compensation payments promised him after a fifty-year delay, or, if he is prominent, he makes a speech in the Swedish Academy.

And he asks the question: what is he bequeathing, what is his spiritual legacy? Has he enriched human knowledge with his tale of suffering? Or has he only born witness to the unimaginable degradation of the human being, in which there is no lesson, and which ought to be forgotten as quickly as possible? I do not see it that way.

I have not changed my opinion that the Holocaust is a trauma of European civilization. And it is becoming a life-and-death matter, whether this trauma lives on as culture or neurosis, in a constructive or destructive form in European societies.

However, all that will be a decision of the future, which I can scarcely hope to influence any longer. I have endeavoured – perhaps it is not sheer self-deception – to perform the existential labour that being an Auschwitz-survivor has thrust upon me as a kind of obligation. I realize what a privilege has been bestowed on me.

I have seen the true visage of this dreadful century, I have gazed into the eye of the Gorgon, and have been able to keep on living. Yet, I knew I would never be able to free myself from the sight; I knew this visage would always hold me captive. Over the decades and one by one I rejected the misleading slogans of a misleading freedom such as "an inexplicable historical error", "cannot be rationalized", and other tautologies of that kind.

They are the gestures of one who wishes to stand above the fray. I have never succumbed to the temptation of self-pity, nor, it may be, to that of true sublimity and divine perspicacity, but I have known from the beginning that my disgrace was not merely a humiliation; it also concealed redemption, if only my heart could be courageous enough to accept this redemption, this peculiarly cruel form of grace, and even to recognize grace at all in such a cruel form.

And if you now ask me what still keeps me here on this earth, what keeps me alive, then, I would answer without any hesitation: love.

J. M. COETZEE
2003

INTRODUCTION

John Maxwell Coetzee was born in Cape Town, South Africa, on 9 February 1940, the elder of two children. His mother was a primary school teacher. His father was trained as an attorney, but practiced as such only intermittently; during the years 1941–45 he served with the South African forces in North Africa and Italy.

Though Coetzee's parents were not of British descent, the language spoken at home was English.

Coetzee received his primary schooling in Cape Town and in the nearby town of Worcester. For his secondary education he attended a school in Cape Town run by a Catholic order, the Marist Brothers. He matriculated in 1956.

Coetzee entered the University of Cape Town in 1957, and in 1960 and 1961 graduated successively with honours degrees in English and mathematics. He spent the years 1962–65 in England, working as a computer programmer while doing research for a thesis on the English novelist Ford Madox Ford.

In 1963 he married Philippa Jubber (1939–1991). They had two children, Nicolas (1966–1989) and Gisela (b. 1968).

In 1965 Coetzee entered the graduate school of the University of Texas at Austin, and in 1968 graduated with a PhD in English, linguistics, and Germanic languages. His doctoral dissertation was on the early fiction of Samuel Beckett.

For three years (1968–71) Coetzee was assistant professor of English at the State University of New York in Buffalo.

After an application for permanent residence in the United States was denied, he returned to South Africa. From 1972 until 2000 he held a series of positions at the University of Cape Town, the last of them as Distinguished Professor of Literature.

Between 1984 and 2003 he also taught frequently in the United States: at the State University of New York, Johns Hopkins University, Harvard University, Stanford University, and the University of Chicago, where for six years he was a member of the Committee on Social Thought.

Coetzee began writing fiction in 1969. His first book, *Dusklands*, was published in South Africa in 1974. *In the Heart of the Country* (1977) won South Africa's then principal literary award, the CNA Prize, and was published in Britain and the USA.

Waiting for the Barbarians (1980) received international notice. His reputation was confirmed by *Life & Times of Michael K* (1983), which won Britain's Booker Prize. It was followed by *Foe* (1986), *Age of Iron* (1990), *The Master of Petersburg* (1994), and *Disgrace* (1999), which again won the Booker Prize.

Coetzee also wrote two fictionalized memoirs, *Boyhood* (1997) and *Youth* (2002). *The Lives of Animals* (1999) is a fictionalized lecture, later absorbed into *Elizabeth Costello* (2003).

White Writing (1988) is a set of essays on South African literature and culture. *Doubling the Point* (1992) consists of essays and interviews with David Attwell. *Giving Offense* (1996) is a study of literary censorship. *Stranger Shores* (2001) collects his later literary essays.

Coetzee has also been active as a translator of Dutch and Afrikaans literature.

In 2002 Coetzee emigrated to Australia. He lives with his partner Dorothy Driver in Adelaide, South Australia, where he holds an honorary position at the University of Adelaide.

He was awarded the Nobel Prize for Literature in 2003.

PRIZE ACCEPTANCE SPEECH

J. M. Coetzee's speech at the Nobel Banquet, December 10, 2003

Your Majesties,
Your Royal Highnesses,

Ladies and Gentlemen;

Distinguished Guests, Friends

The other day, suddenly, out of the blue, while we were talking about something completely different, my partner Dorothy burst out as follows: "On the other hand," she said, "*on the other hand*, how proud your mother would have been! What a pity she isn't still alive! And your father too! How proud they would have been of you!"

"Even prouder than of my son the doctor?" I said. "Even prouder than of my son the professor?"

"Even prouder."

"If my mother were still alive," I said, "she would be ninety-nine and a half. She would probably have senile dementia. She would not know what was going on around her."

But of course I missed the point. Dorothy was right. My mother would have been bursting with pride. *My son the Nobel Prize winner*. And for whom, anyway, do we do the things that lead to Nobel Prizes if not for our mothers?

"*Mommy, Mommy, I won a prize!*"

"*That's wonderful, my dear. Now eat your carrots before they get cold.*"

Why must our mothers be ninety-nine and long in the grave before we can come running home with the prize that will make up for all the trouble we have been to them?

To Alfred Nobel, 107 years in the grave, and to the Foundation that so faithfully administers his will and that has created this magnificent evening for us, my heartfelt gratitude. To my parents, how sorry I am that you cannot be here.

Thank you.

ORHAN PAMUK
2006

INTRODUCTION

Orhan Pamuk was born 7 June 1952 in Istanbul into a prosperous, secular middle-class family. His father was an engineer as were his paternal uncle and grandfather. It was this grandfather who founded the family's fortune. Growing up, Pamuk was set on becoming a painter. He graduated from Robert College then studied architecture at Istanbul Technical University and journalism at Istanbul University.

He wrote about this in his first published novel, a family chronicle entitled *Cevdet Bey Ve Ogullari* (1982), which in the spirit of Thomas Mann follows the development of a family over three generations.

His second novel, *Sessiz Ev* (1983; *The House of Silence,* 1998), uses five different narrator perspectives to describe a situation in which several family members visit their ageing grandmother at a popular seaside resort with Turkey teetering on the brink of civil war.

Pamuk's writing has become known for its play with identities and doubles. The issue appears in his novel *Kara Kitap* (1990; The Black Book, 1995) in which the protagonist searches the hubbub of Istanbul for his vanished wife and her half-brother, with whom he later exchanges identities. Frequent references to the mystic tradition of the East make it natural to see this in a Sufi perspective. *Kara Kitap* represented a definite break with the governing social realism in Turkish literature. It provoked debate in Turkey not least through its Sufism references. Pamuk based his screenplay for the film *Gizli Yüz* (1992) on the novel.

Pamuk has published a collection of essays, *Öteki Renkler : Seçme Yazilar Ve Bir Hikâye* (1999), and a city portrait, *Istanbul : Hatiralar Ve Sehir* (2003; *Istanbul : Memories and the City,* 2006).

Literary Prizes and Awards: Milliyet Roman Yarismasi Ödülü (1979, shared with Mehmet Eroglu), Orhan Kemal Roman Ödülü (1983), Madarali roman Ödülü (1984), the Independent Award for Foreign Fiction (1990), Prix de la Découverte Européenne (1991), Prix France Culture (1995), Prix du Meilleur Livre Étranger (2002), Premio Grinzane Cavour (2002), the IMPAC Dublin Award (2003), Ricarda-Huch-Preis (2005), Der Friedenspreis des Deutschen Buchhandels (2005), Prix Médicis étranger (2005), Prix Méditerranée Étranger (2006).

PRIZE ACCEPTANCE SPEECH

Orhan Pamuk's speech at the Nobel Banquet, December 10, 2006

Why do you write? This is the question I've been asked most often in my writing career. Most of the time they mean this: What is the point, why do you give your time to this strange and impossible activity? Why do you write... You have to give an excuse, an apology for writing... This is how I have felt every time I've heard this question. But every time I give a different answer... Sometimes I say: I do not know why I write, but it definitely makes me feel good. I hope you feel the same when you read me! Sometimes I say that I am angry, and that is why I write. Most of the time the urge is to be alone in a room, so that is why I write. In my childhood I wanted to be a painter. I painted every day. I still have that childish feeling of joy and happiness whenever I write. I write to pursue that old childish happiness and that is why for me literature and writing are inextricably linked with happiness, or the lack of it... unhappiness. In my childhood, I felt happy, painted a lot, and all the grown ups were constantly smiling at me. Everybody was gentle, polite and tender. I wrote all about this in my autobiographical book, *Istanbul.* After the publication of *Istanbul,* some people asked me this question: Aren't you a bit young to write your autobiography? I kept my silence. Literature is about happiness, I wanted to say, about preserving your childishness all your life, keeping the child in you alive... Now, some years later, I've received this great prize. This time the same people begin asking another question: Aren't you a bit young to get the Nobel Prize? Actually the question I've heard most often since the news of this prize reached me is: How does it feel to get the Nobel Prize? I say, oh! It feels good. All the grown ups are constantly smiling at me. Suddenly everybody is again gentle, polite and tender. In fact, I almost feel like a prince. I feel like a child. Then for a moment, I realize why sometimes I have felt so angry. This prize, which brought back to me the tender smiles of my childhood and the kindness of the strangers, should have been given to me not at this age (54) which some think is too young, but much much earlier, even earlier than my childhood, perhaps two weeks after I was born, so that I could have enjoyed the princely feeling of being a child all my life. In fact now... come to think of it... That is why I write and why I will continue to write.

HERTA MÜLLER
2009

INTRODUCTION

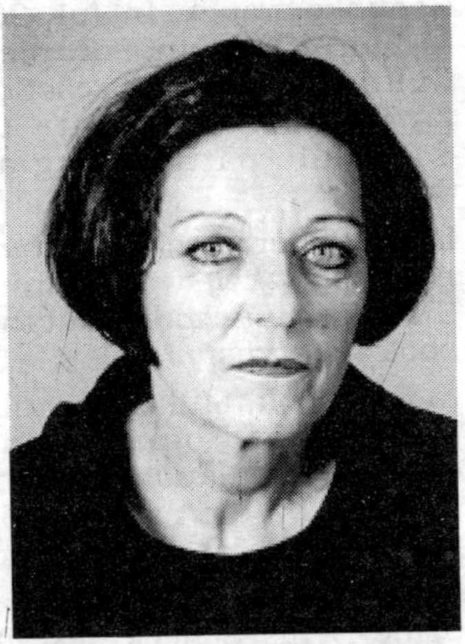

Müller was born in Nicchidorf, a historically German-speaking village in the Romanian Banat in western Romania. The daughter of Banat Swabian farmers, her family was part of Romania's German minority.

Her grandfather had been a wealthy farmer and merchant. Her father served in the Waffen SS and her mother survived five years in a Gulag forced labour camp in the Ukraine (then part of the Soviet Union) after World War II, sharing the fate of around 100,000 ethnic Germans deported from Romania to forced labor camps in the Soviet Union.

Her native language is German; only in grammar school did she learn Romanian. She was a student of German studies and Romanian literature at the Timi_oara University.

In 1976, Müller began working as a translator for an engineering factory, but was dismissed in 1979 for her refusal to cooperate with the Securitate, the Communist regime's secret police.

After her dismissal she initially earned a living by teaching kindergarten and giving private German lessons. Her first book, *Niederungen* (*Nadirs*), was published in Romania in German in 1982, in a state-censored version.

The book was about a child's view of the German-cultural Banat. Müller was a member of Aktionsgruppe Banat, a group of

German-speaking writers in Romania who supported freedom of speech over the censorship they faced under Ceau_escu's government, and her works, including *The Land of Green Plums*, deal with these issues. Radu Tinu, the Securitate officer in charge of her case, denies that she ever suffered any persecutions.

After being refused permission to emigrate to West Germany in 1985, Müller was finally allowed to leave along with her husband, novelist Richard Wagner, in 1987, and they settled in West Berlin, where they still live. In the following years she accepted lectureships at universities in Germany and abroad.

Müller was elected to membership in the German Academy for Writing and Poetry in 1995, and other honorary positions followed. In 1997 she withdrew from the PEN centre of Germany in protest of its merger with the former German Democratic Republic branch. In July 2008, Müller sent a critical open letter to Horia-Roman Patapievici, president of the Romanian Cultural Institute in reaction to the moral and financial support given by the institute to two former informants of the Securitate participating at the Romanian-German Summer School.

In 2009, her novel *Everything I Possess I Carry With Me* (German: *Atemschaukel*) was nominated for the German Book Prize (*Deutscher Buchpreis*) but the prize was won by Kathrin Schmidt's book *Du stirbst nicht*.

In this book, Müller describes the journey of a young man to a gulag in the Soviet Union as an example of the fate of the German population in Transylvania after World War II. It was inspired by the experience of poet Oskar Pastior, whose oral memories she had made notes of, but also by what happened to her own mother.

Critic Denis Scheck described visiting Müller at her home in Berlin and seeing that her working desk contained a drawer full of single letters cut from a newspaper she had entirely destroyed. Realising that she used the letters "to recombine her own literary texts", he felt he had "entered the workshop of a true poet".

The Swedish Academy awarded the 2009 Nobel Prize in Literature to Müller "who, with the concentration of poetry and the frankness of prose, depicts the landscape of the dispossessed.". The spokesman of the Swedish Academy compared Müllers style and her use of German as a minority language with Franz Kafka and pointed out the influence of Kafka on Müller. The award coincided with the 20th anniversary of the fall of communism. Michael Krüger, head of Müller's publishing house, stated: "By giving the award to

Herta Müller, who grew up in a German-speaking minority in Romania, the committee has recognized an author who refuses to let the inhumane side of life under communism be forgotten" However, the award has met with some criticism, mostly in the USA, where the media had hoped for an American win. Prior to the award, Müller was little known outside European intellectuals and literatury critics. Nevertheless she had already been translated in over 20 languages, received many prizes, and was named multiple times a favorite for the Nobel prize.

PRIZE ACCEPTANCE SPEECH

Herta Müller's speech at the Nobel Banquet, December 10, 2009

Your Majesties

Your Royal Highnesses

Ladies and Gentlemen

Dear Friends

The trajectory that leads from a child tending cows in the valley to the Stockholm City Hall is a strange one. Here, too, (as is often the case), I am standing beside myself.

It was only against my mother's will that I attended the preparatory high school in the city. She wanted me to become a seamstress in the village. She knew that if I moved to the city I would become corrupted. And I was. I started to read books. The village seemed more and more to me like a box in which a person was born, married and died. All the people in the village inhabited an older time, they were born old. I thought: sooner or later you have to leave the village if you want to grow young. In the village everyone cowered before the state, but among themselves and towards each other they were obsessively controlling, to the point of self-destruction. The same mix of cowardice and control could be found throughout the city as well. Private cowardice to the point of self-destruction, state control to the point of breaking the individual. That is perhaps the shortest way to describe daily life during the dictatorship.

Fortunately I made some friends in the city, a handful of young writers from the *Aktionsgruppe Banat*. Without them I wouldn't have read or written any books at all. More importantly: these friends were absolutely essential. Had it not been for them I wouldn't have been able to stand the repression. Today I am thinking of these friends, including the ones in the cemetery – the ones that the Romanian secret service has on its conscience.

I saw many people break down. I was on the verge of doing so myself, but shortly before that happened I was able to leave Romania. I'd already had a great deal of luck, all undeserved, since luck is not something that can be deserved. *Happiness* may perhaps be shared. But not luck, sadly. Now, standing here beside myself in Stockholm, I'm very lucky once again. Because this prize helps both those who lived through the kind of repression that aims to break human beings and those who, thank God, did not have to: the ones to remember what they experienced, and the others to bear these things in mind.

Because to this very day there are dictatorships of every stripe. Some go on forever, always frightening us anew, such as Iran.

Others, such as Russia and China, don cloaks of respectability; they liberalize their economies, but human rights remain firmly in the grip of Stalinism or Maoism. And then there are the half-democracies of Eastern Europe, which since 1989 have been putting on and taking off their respectable cloaks so often that they're practically in tatters.

Literature can't change all of that. But it can – and this is in hindsight – use language to invent a truth that shows what happens in us and around us when values become derailed.

Literature speaks with everyone individually – it is personal property that stays inside our heads. And nothing speaks to us as forcefully as a book, which expects nothing in return, other than that we think and feel.

I'd like to thank the Swedish Academy and the Nobel Foundation – many thanks.

Translated by Philip Boehm

MARIO VARGAS LLOSA
2010

INTRODUCTION

Jorge Mario Pedro Vargas Llosa, 1st Marquis of Vargas Llosa (born March 28, 1936) is a Peruvian-Spanish writer, politician, journalist, essayist, and Nobel Prize laureate. Vargas Llosa is one of Latin America's most significant novelists and essayists, and one of the leading authors of his generation.

He was awarded the 2010 Nobel Prize in Literature "for his cartography of structures of power and his trenchant images of the individual's resistance, revolt, and defeat".

Mario Vargas Llosa was born to a middle-class family on March 28, 1936, in the Peruvian provincial city of Arequipa. He was the only child of Ernesto Vargas Maldonado and Dora Llosa Ureta (the former a bus driver, the latter the daughter of an old criollo family), who separated a few months before his birth.

Shortly after Mario's birth, his father revealed that he was having an affair with a German woman; consequently, Mario has two younger half-brothers: Enrique and Ernesto Vargas.

Vargas Llosa rose to fame in the 1960s with novels such as *The Time of the Hero* (*La ciudad y los perros*, literally *The City and the Dogs*, 1963/1966), *The Green House* (*La casa verde*, 1965/1968), and the monumental *Conversation in the Cathedral* (*Conversación en la catedral*, 1969/1975). He writes prolifically across an array of literary genres, including literary criticism and journalism.

His novels include comedies, murder mysteries, historical novels, and political thrillers. Several, such as *Captain Pantoja and the Special Service* (1973/1978) and *Aunt Julia and the Scriptwriter* (1977/1982), have been adapted as feature films.

When Vargas Llosa was fourteen, his father sent him to the Leoncio Prado Military Academy in Lima. A year before his graduation, Vargas Llosa began working as an amateur journalist for local newspapers.

He withdrew from the military academy and finished his studies in Piura, where he worked for the local newspaper, *La Industria*, and witnessed the theatrical performance of his first dramatic work, *La huida del Inca.*

In 1953, during the government of Manuel A. Odría, Vargas Llosa enrolled in Lima's National University of San Marcos, the oldest university of the Americas, to study law and literature. He married Julia Urquidi, his maternal uncle's sister-in-law, in 1955 at the age of 19; she was 10 years older.

Vargas Llosa began his literary career in earnest in 1957 with the publication of his first short stories, "The Leaders" ("Los jefes") and "The Grandfather" ("El abuelo"), while working for two Peruvian newspapers. Their marriage lasted only a few more years, ending in divorce in 1964.

A year later, Vargas Llosa married his first cousin, Patricia Llosa, with whom he had three children: Álvaro Vargas Llosa (born 1966), a writer and editor; Gonzalo (born 1967), a businessman; and Morgana (born 1974), a photographer.

PRIZE ACCEPTANCE SPEECH

Mario Vargas Llosa 's speech at the Nobel Banquet, December 10, 2010

I am a storyteller, so before I propose a toast I will tell you a story.

Once upon a time, there was a boy who learned to read at the age of five. This changed his life. Owing to the adventure tales he read, he discovered a way to escape from the poor house, the poor country and the poor reality in which he lived, and to journey to wonderful, mesmerizing places peopled with the most beautiful beings and the most surprising things, where every day and every night brought a more intense, more thrilling more unusual form of bliss.

He so enjoyed reading stories that one day this boy, who was now a young man, took to making them up himself and writing them. He had a hard time doing it, but it brought him pleasure and he delighted in writing tales as much as he delighted in reading them.

The character in my story, however, was very aware that the real world was one thing and the fancy world of dreams and literature quite another, and that the latter only came to light when he read and wrote stories. The rest of the time, it vanished.

Until one day, in the wee hours of the morning, the protagonist of my story received a mysterious call in which a gentleman with a name that defied all pronunciation announced to him that he had won a prize and that in order to receive it he would have to travel to a place called Stockholm, the capital of a land called Sweden (or something of the sort).

To his total bewilderment, my character then started to experience in real life one of those stories that until then he had only found in the unreal and ideal realm of literature. He suddenly felt like the pauper must have felt when he was confused with the prince in Mark Twain's The Prince and the Pauper.

He is still there, quite startled, not knowing whether he is dreaming or fully awake, whether what is happening is for real or a lie, whether what is occurring is life or literature, because the border that separates the two seems to have totally vanished.

Dear friends, now I can propose the toast I had promised. Let us toast to Sweden, that strange kingdom that seems to have performed, for a privileged few, the miracle of turning life into literature and literature into life.

Cheers (skål) and thank you very much!

MO YAN
2012

INTRODUCTION

Mo Yan (a pseudonym for Guan Moye) was born in 1955 and grew up in Gaomi in Shandong province in north-eastern China. His parents were farmers. As a twelve-year-old during the Cultural Revolution he left school to work, first in agriculture, later in a factory. In 1976 he joined the People's Liberation Army and during this time began to study literature and write. His first short story was published in a literary journal in 1981.

In his writing Mo Yan draws on his youthful experiences and on settings in the province of his birth. The book consists of five stories that unfold and interweave in Gaomi in several turbulent decades in the 20th century, with depictions of bandit culture, the Japanese occupation and the harsh conditions endured by poor farm workers. Red Sorghum was successfully filmed in 1987, directed by Zhang Yimou. The novel Tiantang suantai zhi ge (1988, in English The Garlic Ballads 1995) and his satirical Jiuguo (1992, in English The Republic of Wine 2000) have been judged subversive because of their sharp criticism of contemporary Chinese society.

PRIZE ACCEPTANCE SPEECH

Writer Per Wästberg delivering the Presentation Speech for the 2012 Nobel Prize in Literature at the Stockholm Concert Hall.

Your Majesties, Your Royal Highnesses, Esteemed Nobel Laureates, Ladies and Gentlemen,

Mo Yan is a poet who tears down stereotypical propaganda posters, elevating the individual from an anonymous human mass. Using ridicule and sarcasm Mo Yan attacks history and its falsifications as well as deprivation and political hypocrisy. Playfully and with ill-disguised delight, he reveals the murkiest aspects of human existence, almost inadvertently finding images of strong symbolic weight.

North-eastern Gaomi county embodies China's folk tales and history. Few real journeys can surpass these to a realm where the clamour of donkeys and pigs drowns out the voices of the people's commissars and where both love and evil assume supernatural proportions.

Mo Yan's imagination soars across the entire human existence. He is a wonderful portrayer of nature; he knows virtually all there is to know about hunger, and the brutality of China's 20th century has probably never been described so nakedly, with heroes, lovers, torturers, bandits - and especially, strong, indomitable mothers. He shows us a world without truth, common sense or compassion, a world where people are reckless, helpless and absurd.

Proof of this misery is the cannibalism that recurs in China's history. In Mo Yan, it stands for unrestrained consumption, excess, rubbish, carnal pleasures and the indescribable desires that only he can attempt to elucidate beyond all tabooed limitations.

In his novel Republic of Wine, the most exquisite of delicacies is a roasted three-year-old. Boys have become exclusive foodstuff. The girls, neglected, survive. The irony is directed at China's family policy, because of which female foetuses are aborted on an astronomic scale: girls aren't even good enough to eat. Mo Yan has written an entire novel, Frog, about this.

Mo Yan's stories have mythical and allegorical pretensions and turn all values on their heads. We never meet that ideal citizen who was a standard feature in Mao's China. Mo Yan's characters bubble with vitality and take even the most amoral steps and measures to fulfil their lives and burst the cages they have been confined in by fate and politics.

Instead of communism's poster-happy history, Mo Yan describes a past that, with his exaggerations, parodies and derivations from myths and folk tales, is a convincing and scathing revision of fifty years of propaganda.

In his most remarkable novel, Big Breasts and Wide Hips, where a female perspective dominates, Mo Yan describes the Great Leap Forward and the Great Famine of 1960 in stinging detail. He mocks the revolutionary pseudo-science that tried to inseminate sheep with rabbit sperm, all the while dismissing doubters as right-wing elements. The novel ends with the new capitalism of the '90s with fraudsters becoming rich on beauty products and trying to produce a Phoenix through cross-fertilisation.

In Mo Yan, a forgotten peasant world arises, alive and well, before our eyes, sensually scented even in its most pungent vapours, startlingly merciless but tinged by joyful selflessness. Never a dull moment. The author knows everything and can describe everything – all kinds of handicraft, smithery, construction, ditch-digging, animal husbandry, the tricks of guerrilla bands. He seems to carry all human life on the tip of his pen.

He is more hilarious and more appalling than most in the wake of Rabelais and Swift — in our time, in the wake of García Marquez. His spice blend is a peppery one. On his broad tapestry of China's last hundred years, there are neither dancing unicorns nor skipping maidens. But he paints life in a pigsty in such a way that we feel we have been there far too long. Ideologies and reform movements may come and go but human egoism and greed remain. So Mo Yan defends small individuals against all injustices – from Japanese occupation to Maoist terror and today's production frenzy.

For those who venture to Mo Yan's home district, where bountiful virtue battles the vilest cruelty, a staggering literary adventure awaits. Has ever such an epic spring flood engulfed China and the rest of the world? In Mo Yan's work, world literature speaks with a voice that drowns out most contemporaries.

The Swedish Academy congratulates you. I call on you to accept the 2012 Nobel Prize for Literature from the hand of His Majesty the King.

~~~
~~~